written in a room

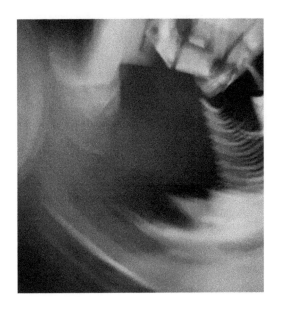

published in the sky

"You got me wrong says he.
The sun don't shine in your
TV." - *Daniel Johnston*

To S.D., for showing me Kurt Vonnegut - and to Dad, for taking me fishing

Cover art by Rita Cabrito

ORBO AND THE GODHEAD

by Luke Delin

I

Orbo, or what would become of Orbo at least,

was — though inversely — perhaps most reminiscent in that noon June sun of 1987, suspended in a sea of cerulean, a sea of clouds and nixies in lower earth orbit. Deep down below, a bearded dame happened upon swallowing a whistle, if you can believe it. Sighing silver and such. To rectify the situation, a rickety ambulance had come down the rutted road just off from the platz an elongated while after the choking that ensued had disturbed the village folk enough for the day. The whistle, which was small but weighty, hummed bizarrely from her esophagus. Though whistle ingestion was fairly uncommon, the paramedic assured her it was a routine operation. Only was it a magnetic whistle, the medic asked, because that might cause some problems, to which the bearded dame in the now unveiled red goldy babushka replied no it was not a magnetic one, it was an old memento from her father and it was brass. Was she going to die, she asked the woman, the whistling syncing to the word die in a real surreal fashion. The medic checked her throat with a little plastic flashlight, her rubbery fuchsia gloves prying into Hazel Kahn's chapped and ageing mouth, the whistles disembodied and staccato. Nearby, beachwards, way up from the North Sea, a school of bottlenose dolphins high on pufferfish save a small fat German boy from a hammerhead. They could not, however, save the lad's ice cream cone, and were puzzled in long debate about how to even schlep it back to him, as reprieve for the kid. And for it not to be wet. The lad himself — after a perplexed stare into the Düsum shore when the school of dolphins rang its bells and swam off to find more pufferfish so they could laugh at the water of gunmetal grey and their strange silky faces in the reflection of the surface — abandoned all hope of that strawberry ice cream. It kind of put a downer on his whole being saved from the hammerhead. Eclipsed it somehow. He couldn't just go to the stand and say he dropped it and could he have another, because he had done that so many times before, mendaciously, said he dropped it when he didn't. At first, in lieu of alms, the little bunko had made it work invariably well, though after near a dozen attempts at this in only the space of a few days, the man and his daughter who were stationed at the Eisstand began to see the evidence in his little fat gut, sometimes remnants of cream still ridiculously on his face as he made the con. I dropped mine again, he would say, then adding 'yet' to mix it up. Yet again, he would say. The odds of this! he would belch. It was like a racket. He was The Boy Who Cried Dropped Ice Cream. Now no one had believed him when he really did drop it. In the sea. From the hammer. He was The Lad Who Screamed Cream. Way worse than a hungry wolf at the door. Or a hungry hammer. He was the hungry one. An intercontinental calamity, as far as he was concerned.

He wondered if the old woman in the gilt red hood who had been choking and crawling around on the floor attracting birdlife was still there as she had been a few hours ago, but as he stepped up the sandy beach to the incline of the rocky road beyond he saw she was no longer accounted for. The birds had vamoosed, too. Maybe, he thunk to himself, she was actually dead, and sort of seeped into the earth. Babushka and all. Maybe that's how people die, he thunk. You just get all invisible and such. Sink into the earth. I mean, he had never seen anybody die before. And that woman was obviously in a bad way, hunched on all fours choking and attracting birdlife, with no one even seeming to want to help her amid the arrhythmic shriek. He thought maybe it had to do with the beard and not the whistle. Like, for instance, at school, there was this girl who had an improbable mustache above her upper lip, Lyra Castellanos, and he remembered how quite a few of the boys and even more of the girls had mocked her mustache and by all accounts practically expedited her own bucket kick at the harrowing age of twelve years old. He spent a lot of time thinking about it, this day, this dusk, skipping stones he'd found by the roadside and watching them bounce over the water's top. After she went — it was about five years or so before the fall of the Berlin Wall — Elbert would often walk up the hillock at the north of the village and go to her gravestone and tear up a little, because he hated what the kids from school had said to her and how they drove her to it. In a way, they were just like the Wall. He would go all the way to the hillock and go to the stone and just, cry. It wasn't her fault she had a mustache. The fact that she never shaved it off, never tried to hide it at school, was what made him feel she must have been a very defiant sort of girl. And it was gut wrenching to still be around these demons, these Walls who had tortured her into it — while she herself, maybe the only true angel in the joint, was gone forever. Sunk into the earth. Sunk way down. A beauteous starscape at the bottom of the sea, the mustache growing to paranatural levels, wrapping round her pallid cheeks, unseen and sarcophagal.

It was the same day of the hammer attack when he returned to her stone once more. Had to do something to take his mind off the hunger. He saw the name and he saw the date. The old name and date.

"Hey, Lyra."

"..."

"Do you mind if I say something I've been meaning to say, Lyra?"

"..."

"You know, not everybody hated you at school. It's true. There's this one kid who got real sad when he heard. Elbert. Elbert Mann. That's me. I don't know if I believe in ghosts but if you were a ghost then we could talk, right?"

"..."

"You can see me cry. I'm not embarrassed."

"..."

"I think I really liked you or something. More than ice cream."

"..."

"What's death like, Lyra? Are you alone down there? Is everybody alone?"

"..."

"I nearly got eaten by a shark today. Anyway, here's some lilies." He gently placed the flowers so they leant against the granite block. "If you like them I can bring more, I can come every day if you want."

"..."

"You know, you're a really good listener. Nobody listens to me."

"..."

"{Sneezes.}"

"..."

"What's death like, Lyra? Is it alright down there? Are there dolphins? Do people like your mustache? You know, I hope they do. I hope your head has a halo, because you're an angel I think. Do you like the lilies? I got them because you always had that lily on your lapel, remember? I was smelling them when I took them from my Ma's room. I know I shouldn't have taken them because Ma would kill me if she found out. But maybe then I'd be a ghost, too."

"..."

"Hey, Lyra?"

Out by the back door of a certain custodial

closet in Blighty which for some reason wasn't actually clean
and never had been, at last away from all the shiny people
demanding their previous number of towels squared for
bodies which were not only shiny but sort of oozy and
vague like what you see when you shove a digit or
protuberance in your optics, or even just stare at a good old
lightbulb or the lume of the vinyl sun — Buck Da Luz, in his
black Illumine polo, leant against a tree he couldn't name on
smoko with twenty nine year old coworker Sophia Flint out
the rear exit of the Illumine Spa Resort and Hotel. There
was a slight buzzing sound coming from Sophia's
Mindphone. Sophia Flint had hair the hue of a raven that
had somehow managed to fork out for purple highlights. In

the night it almost made her look bald because the hair was so dark and it was so dark outside that the hair and the night like joined together as one entity. Buck wanted to say he didn't know where the hair started and the night began, but refrained, thinking she might think it was a romantical statement, which it most definitely wasn't. It was more like an observation of what he could actually see. Or not see. Their low lit view overlooked the upslope of the dewy hill beyond the swollen car park, not a single jalopy in sight. They were, after all, quite rich, the guests — they had to be just to pay the hulkish fees to get in, after all — and them lot tended to avoid jalopies like the plague (or a flyer guy). This was unlike the cleaning crew whose mode of transport was nothing but a run down bus that a lot of the time made them late for work. In fact, it was quite good that it was usually late, since if it wasn't late they could claim that it was and on the whole be believed. But it really was late most of the time. Da Luz and Flint were both heavy smokers and would have to ditch their unfinished snouts if the manager, or some poor bootlicker of aforementioned manager, was walking through the grounds for some reason or treason. All clandestine and such. The boss of the joint, a one Kate Road, was a brass chapping bitch, Buck said to Flint, whispering in case the Road was behind him. Sophia felt for her vitiligo'd chin (a milkwhite mark about the size of a two quider that rested under her otherwise tawny right cheek) and nodded her head emphatically, but in a way that was like the gesticulatory equivalent of the phrase *Cheers For That, Einstein* or *No Shit, Sherlock* or *And Penguin Are Interested?* or *Me Oh My* or *Does The President Know?* or even good old *In Other News, The Moon Is Round (And Thereby Other Moons And Planetary And Stellar Objects Through A Unifying Element Of Gravitational Force That Over A Large Enough Mass Will Tend To A Spheroidal Shape).*

The Road — a nickname Sophia coined and which Buck liked to repeat, because it signified beauteously how dull and arduous she was to them — really had a penchant for materialising during smoko. Kept saying they smoked too much and went off on smoko too much. Made them bust a gut if anything. There was, of course, a kind of unalloyed joy in seeing how many smokos you could get away with without being fuego'd, though only two was pushing it according to the Road, and laughing about it together, Buck and Flint; tapping ash down onto rain soaked and snow capped and sleet strewn and hail hammered concrete together late in the nightly twilit evenings, in tow as usual the anarchic ad hoc sign upon the dwarfish wooden rear door on which was scribed ON SMOKO, intended to be there at all times for matters of smoko ease.

Everybody at the Illumine Spa Resort, except the staff of the gaff, resembles some sort of towel clad apparition. Just drifting around. Chucking their towels and grabbing another. They're like hermit crabs looking for ever more sturdy shells. It's partly due to the obsessive restocking of clean towels done by a towel guy who studies extractive metallurgy and theories of transmutational matter in his spare time. *His* idea is that if he's constantly around water here in the Resort, what with all the pools and saunas and showers and toilets he has to clean, then it only makes sense to juxtapose his wet wrought ways on the weekend against glowing hot metal of metallurgy on the weekdays, to equalise the ontological temperature and such. The guy's name is Hilton Dax. He's a lamppost in a forest most of the time. His great grandfather was a tree. You know? He's just a leaf on a big mad tree, a big mad tree of genealogy. He's the air sometimes too, like his great grandmother. We'll all be invisible one day, Hilton reckons. Like the wind and like the spoken word, and like our great grandfathers and our great grandmothers. Like a dream in our heads that no one else knows about. Invisible like that. It's not all perfect though. Before it all, you have to live a life. But in that life they give you a few dreams sometimes, if you're polite and don't attack them with a ladle. The dream of course becomes a nightmare when you can't escape it. That's called madness by the way. In order to escape, and it is achievable, you must revert the nightmare back into a dream.

He wants to die happy, you know. He doesn't want to live happy. He wants to die happy. Wouldn't that be topshelf? Just having lived so damn long and carpe diem'd that mother to hell and back that you're actually *glad* to get off the Ride once and for all and now you're not in heaven nor the underworld but you do see the universe, its energy, and you can just return to the universe, gladly, a topshelf sedation like that calm peaceful void of before-you-existed times. Pre Dasein. Pre paranoia. Hilton believes on some level he could understand how it might feel to not exist, being a towel guy and all. And because he already had a before-he-existed time before. There had to be a before, because the rents were around when he wasn't — Mr. and Mrs. Dax — so there had to be something going on, before he came. Before Dasein. Before paranoia. Before towels. It didn't even matter if time didn't quote-unquote move.

There was still a before. Before the ore got smelted, as it were. He was already there once. We all were. Or not there rather. There in the not-there-ness. What's new? What's the big deal? It's possibly just like going to sleep except you stay asleep for all of eternity. Ruddy impressive if you actually stop to think about it. Returning to eternity. Topshelf. The catch unfortunately is being unable to brag about it at dinner parties. Dax thinks if they could somehow do it, dead people would probably clad themselves in garbs that read: I WENT TO ETERNITY AND ALL I GOT WAS THIS GODDAMN T-SHIRT (the expletive pretty much greenlit in the afterlife for some reason).

Out again by the rear exit (still on smoko), whorls of carbon monoxide caressed the canvas of the night as Da Luz noticed Flint had the beginnings of jowls from yawning so much. Yawning cools down your brain, she says to him. It cools down your brain. In January.

Apropos of absolutely bloody nothing, some uninvited fruit bats decided to rock up and frazzled the custodians mad leaving Da Luz fanning to hell and Flint's MP to glitch momentarily as she owl spun her head — flicking her butt and nearly lighting a poor mother up before they all flapped away as quick as they arrived. It was like they too were trying to get away from working. Buck made a smoke circle and then failed to repeat the action, trying to line it up with the moon. Flint seemed to be chaining perpetually on the same superking after the kerfuffle had left an immense container of silence, bar the hum of the hotel and the buzz of devices. One silvery cloud encompassed a near monopoly in the air above. No SkyScreens around for now.

Da Luz thought Flint looked wraithlike tonight but made a special effort not to tell her she looked wraithlike. They inhaled and exhaled without exchanging any more words, such was their preferred arrangement at the end of the night. It was the kind of silence that was okay to endure, here on smoko out the back door of the cleaning cupboard, the sky an empyrean mosaic of jewels on a blanket of space and time. Flint seemed to almost hover off the ground to Buck, eventually opining that she was jealous of them, the bats, that she wanted to know what it was like to conk out hanging upside down. Buck, saying nothing in reply but not sourly, deaded his rollup and went reluctantly inside to clean the giant poolside windows he was meant to clean forty five minutes previously. Prior to his shoving off, he finally turned his MP on (Buck always had it on during shifts, and off during smoko) and mentioned something about a new recruit, a cleaner, as he stuffed his tobacco pouch in a back pocket. His shadow before it tapered away looked to Flint like a strange robot in the ground. She chucked her own last remaining cig and crushed the butt with her plimsoll, which happened to be right on the robot's head, for Da Luz had still not yet left the closet and was seeming to loiter in there. The bland hum coming from the Hotel and Spa beyond entwined itself with the machinery's. The sky was one colossal blueberry that stretched and shimmered.

III

At the base of the serpentine hill, holding up

some tube of Constitutionally Loco glue almost as if he had removed it from a sheath, as if he was going to bonk the burly men with the tube, Burgess Moon — entombed in a soot soaked KX100 telephone box just below the Illumine Spa Resort and Hotel that jutted out the scalp of the winding hill — strained to hold the grey plastic coated door shut as hard as his musculature would allow him, proceeding to take the Constitutionally Loco's bright red lid off and fire away at the jambs of the door before they could get in. The reason he had the glue on his person, and it was a sort of kismet, the reason, was due to his adopted little brother Ori's request earlier in the day that he grab some for him at the Hub and come down to old Vox's to help fix his time machine (which is what Ori called his clock). He just forgot to give it to him. Some of the glue'd got on the windows he squeezed it so tight. It was stronger than epoxy, hardened in seconds, and it could kill you a horrid way if you were inclined to extraneous nasal enjoyment of the stuff, as the owner and general tagalongs of the nearby skate shop Contused Neil's just down the road were, ever since owner Neil Mosh heard that this hyperglue stuff was not just insane but flat out mythological to honk. It had little skulls on the label, Mosh'd said. Confirmation of Acceptability.

The glue wielder but not glue sniffer had been in the box for hours before they came, snoring like a conked out banshee. He sleepwalked to it for some reason, woke up in there all esoterically. Didn't mind it, though. In fact it was nice. It was an old thing. What they used to call antique stuff. From before when people actually ambulated and had to pick up the remote to turn on the TV. When people even used TVs. Hell, when you got screens in your dome, old things such as the grey KX100 seem like, beautiful. Planted in the asphalt like a spirit of the past. It reminded him of his own. Before the world inbent itself to mindphones, head by ruddy head. More knocking on the KX. It didn't sound like a normal knock. It sounded more like someone was yanking a thunder sheet.

"Can I help you?" he says through the glass.

"Get out, kid."

"Give me two secs." He let go of the door when it was apparent the hardening process had finished, waving at the fluorescent clad men outside. Their faces appeared ghostish.

"I'm twenty seven by the way."

"Yeah. A kid."

"If I'm a kid, then you sir are a nonagenarian."

"Ey? I'm a nonce in a jerrycan, am I?" The man grabbed the door handle — his frustration with the kid clearly riling him up — to no avail.

"I said *nonagenarian*. Boy, this glue really holds up doesn't it."

"Why are you even in there?"

"It's called Constitutionally Loco because the guy who made it is psychotic or something. Have you seen the ad?"

"What bloody ad."

"Those ads for the glue. You know, this lady's wearing a straitjacket and she asks her not so avuncular friend why can't she get it off and the doctor literally points at the glue and smiles a horridly teeth revealing smile at the camera and goes 'the *GLUE!*' And then I swear one time in miniature font at the end it said 'DO NOT NASALLY INGEST, IT'S BONKERED', even though it being only noon on a nondescript Monday. I only saw it because I happened to be using a jeweler's loupe at the time, to check the plant on top of the TV. Remember TVs? God. When everything wasn't straight in your dome, you know?"

"Have no idea what you're talking about."

"I have an MP," says the other hi viz'd fella. "My MP works great."

"You know, even if we can't open the door we can still get it towed all the same? With you inside or not."

"I'm here to get away, is all. Dreadfully hypnagogic. You boys dreadfully hypnagogic?"

"You can't stay in there, kid."

"Tow me. Crane me. Nuke me. I'm not leaving." He held up the tube just like the guy on the advert, all dramatic and optics popping out his skull and did the same barmy teeth thing and eventually one of the guys gave ground and left to smoke, the other cradling his chapped cranium in a claw, dome downcast below the nimbi. It was only slightly warmer in the old phonebox, though Burgess still chattered his teeth and wrapped his collar to as high as it would reach, tremulous as a woofer playing the aural equivalent of an epileptic fit — short of breath and secretly panicked like one who'd come to clock that maybe they didn't have their best thinking cap on as of late, what with hypergluing himself inside a disused telephone box.

"Listen," says the remaining guy, his face faded and blurred behind the glass. "We came to take the KX. It's the last one in the country. Got *government* orders to take down all telephone boxes. But now you've trapped yourself in there like a right plum. We'll need to break the door open."

"Last one in the country? I'll buy it off you. Hold on. I got, lemme see here, I got fif-, no, *six*teen quid." The man from the council declined to reply.

He put the coins back in his right chino pocket, his breath emitting nomad clouds. They meshed into the glassy walls and fogged them up on impact, now meaning he couldn't see the gentlemen or in fact much anything outside. There was a lamppost across the road which ominously shut off its light. An unnoticed barn owl happened to notice it, silently jutting through the darkened air. It was almost like being in a sensory deprivation tank now. It would have been if not for the sensory input of the men from the council babbling and a certain urinary stench in the phonebox. Not his own urine, by the way.

The reason he'd left his flat that night was not merely the somnambulism. It was more that he was trying to evade some sort of ensnarement. Only it was an ensnarement that had already draped the world. It seemed it got to the point if you weren't constantly using a screen of some sort then something had to be wrong with you. They made it out that *you* were the weird one for not getting into the whole MP spirit like they had. Though he'd never once used a mindphone — a term originating from the acronym MIND or Maximum Immersion Neural Device — even the rest of it was too much. It just got too much this night. And his unconscious knew it, judiciously making his lousy self schlep around mid conk just to get away from the screens. It was like they were everywhere or something, everyone constantly watching them too and finding nothing there but still constantly watching. And now with the help of Mindphone Co.'s new building in the environs of North Mupfield and their deal of MPs for everyone in town in gratis, people became the screens they watched. Just ebony mirrors, all of Mupfield. All of everywhere. When they started putting holographic screens in the sky for adverts of the device intermingled with semi famous footballers talking about crisps was when Burgess Moon truly lost it.

He really needed a Boris Johnson but obviously there was no way to reach a toilet. A numero uno was out of the question, too. What the hell had he done. He gazed at the glue. The skulls seemed to wink. He did as best he could to hold in the former Prime Minister and clocked as he took a hand and smothered it like a windshield wiper over the phone box's clouded glass door that the folk were still there. There was even another, with a microphone. Due to the blurring effect of the box, it almost looked like she was holding a gun before he realised he was seeing things when a cameraman with a big old camera apparated behind her. Turned out eventually those things were merely props — they were in fact recording via the MIND.

"Who are you lot?"

"Joy Merchant, reporter for News Straight To Your Head," she says. "Why is this man in there? You know they take out the phones now, so it's just a box?"

"We came to cart it," the man from the council says. "It's the last one left. Found this kid sleeping in there. Snoring like something I've never seen."

"Seemed to be some scene going on is why I came over." The cameraman behind either smiled or grimaced. It was turning code red foggy in the phonebox, the surface lit up strangely resembling diamond shards seen through a plastic toy kaleidoscope. He tried not to exhale so much, and when that didn't pan out he resigned his breaths to the roof. A twenty year old piece of gum hung from one corner like a shell pink string.

"Didn't know people watched the news at four in the morning. Didn't know people did anything at four in the morning."

"It's global. Ever heard of a mindphone? Listen, can I talk to the man in the box? What's his name?"

"It's Burgess," says Burgess from the box. "Burgess Moon."

"Moon. Any relation to Elbert Moon?"

"I'd rather not talk about my dad if that's okay."

"Why are you in there, Burgess?"

"I glued it, mam. With that CL glue."

"Oh. CL?" she says. "Those adverts are awful, aren't they. Why'd you shut yourself in, Mr. Moon?"

"I hate the MPs. The HG screens in the sky. All that stuff has made the people in this town just plain, *weird*. And I realise it's four in the morning and I'm talking inside a phonebox right now, but even so —" He lifted his finger to the ceiling as if to alert an upcoming sneeze which never came out. "There was a Gillette advert on fucking *Pleiades* last night. Oh nuts, sorry. I didn't mean to swear."

"You are allowed."

"I am?" he says, rubbing the glass so he could see her better.

"Well, we wouldn't *ask* you to drop any bombs per se. But it's fine. We actually find the graveyard shift a good time for honesty" — (waves her microphone to the inky empyrean) — "though no, we wouldn't exactly request that you do. Drop bombs, that is."

"Gee, you guys should run for Cabinet."

"You were saying about Gillette?"

"It's just I hate the SkyScreens. I'm bloody sick of it. The MPs too. I needed to go somewhere that was like, old. Like nature or something. You know?"

"And so you chose a phonebox."

"Yes, mam."

"Please. Call me Joy."

"It would be a joy. Sorry. Nervous. I've never been interviewed before." He wiped his frozen nose. The men from the council were gone.

"So are you saying you're protesting the company, glueing yourself shut in here? Even though your father is the man behind the very device? The true creator of the

Mindphone?" The camera eyed him up and down through the glass's condensation. If one had just tuned in, they could be forgiven for thinking this was some kind of paranatural ghost hunting show, him looking all spectral and such.

"I am, Joy. Well, I kinda sleepwalked here but yes now that I think about it yes I am protesting. We need to get rid of the mindphones. It's driving me barmy, and I've never even used the thing. They're everywhere. You ever go on a train or something now? Ever see the people sitting in the seats? They all have them. You can hear the collective whir. Those folk. Get a good look in one of their faces sometime. Dribbling from the mouth. And it's not just this town. It's the whole damn world. A full frontal lobotomy of planet Earth. I mean, I've seen bibs recently, to account for all the surplus of saliva. How I wish I was joshing, Joy." Faraway, on the other side of the equator, a man paranoid of time checks his MP's clock on the home screen once again.

"Some might call you a Luddite, Mr. Moon."

"It's just personally driving me up the wall, Joy. And I don't think I'm alone in that fact. At least, I hope I'm not. I sure as hell hope I'm not."

IV

There's so much time when you're glued in a box. A surplus. And everyone can just see you. And by everyone I mean foxes. In lieu of an actual experience, he had a ruddy old think. Thinking back to when the MP never existed. By the Moons' back garden in the time of the early tens to be specific, where the turtle Napoleon Jr. was planning its Houdini.

"Mum! Burgess's existing!"

"Am not."

"Let go of my hair or I swear to Shiva, B!"

"Kids. Can you cease and desist. I'm trying to finish this."

"What?"

"None of your beeswax. Now hurry up and get to school. We're picking up our new little brother Ori at 4. You're not going to be late. Or I swear to all the deities, nevermind ruddy Shiva."

"He's still breathing. Why do you *breathe* so loud?"

"I didn't sleep because you were singing all damn night."

"I'm sorry that I sleep sing. I'm oh so sorry, B."

"Just trying to piss me off. I swear, I'm glad we're getting a little brother and not another one of you lot. Nuts to girls."

"Said the quinquagenarian virgin."

"Delphine! Enough. Take your brother and walk to school."

"But I don't wanna walk with him."

"I don't wanna walk with *her*."

"Go. Now."

"C'mon. What were you writing, Vox?"

"If you must know, it's a story about a woman who gives birth to the Antichrists. Plural. Now get the heck out of this house and walk each other to school. In fact, run. You're going to be late."

"I don't run," says Del. "It's not my style."

"Power walk, then."

"Why can't we get a lift like Georgina does?"

"Because Georgina's mum isn't a goddamn drunk, Delphine."

"Can't Dad take us?"

"No, he can't," she says, holding her forehead. "He's busy."

"He's *always* busy."

"Then it's a wonder you're his kin. Get. To. Bloody. School." She raised the now empty Lambrini over their heads and clonked them both with the bottle neck, only half gently. It was a sign that the Vox was drunk, so they rubbed their heads and bolted.

On the way — passing the neighbour's magnetic sign that had once read BEWARE OF DOGGO but had since been switched around by an unknown hand so it now read AW GEE ORB OF GOD (and which only three days later would be changed further still (presumably by some competitor of the AW GEE ORB OF GOD guy) to the ever eloquent GAG BEFORE WOOD) — Burgess began power walking in a real audacious manner, making Del sort of laugh but not enough for it to become vocal. He was still existing, the sonofabitch.

As he fled down the street, Delphine hung back to smoke a cigarette from a pack she'd found in the Vox's dresser while she was out power walking off a hangover. The Vox really liked to power walk off her hangovers, she thought it would make her live to one hundred. If she had to bet on it, Del'd probably say the Vox only wanted to live that long so she could rack in a few more decades of drinking.

She fiddled with the candy green lighter, blowing out plumes of cobalt blue that danced all the way to her brother's nostrils. Burgess turned back and started to power walk over to her, again imitating the Vox, going right up to her facial regions.

"What're you doing?"

"What do you think."

"Is that one of the Vox's cigarettes? Boy, you're gonna be in trouble."

"Am I. And how would she find out? Are you going to tell her?"

"I'm not a snitch, D. It's just, those things are real horrid for you."

"Well, it's allowing me not to knock your block off."

"Folk who smoke can get lung cancer."

"Thanks, Columbo."

"Aren't you afraid you'll get it and die?"

"Couldn't care less."

"Bullshit. You care."

"I've always wanted to be a phantasm. Now here's my chance. You gotta take chances wherever you can find them." She pinched his shoulder and made a little smile to him, exhaling more blue. Though she was nearly two years his junior, she was much taller than Burgess and also extremely well versed (for a fourteen year old) in 19th, 20th and 21st Century experimental prose, so they sort of agreed to disagree about who was actually the little sibling. They continued the dreaded walk to school. Burgess realigned the brim of his Russian hat.

"Sawyer told me that when you die your ghost does whatever you were doing when you died. Like for all of infinity."

"This Sawyer sounds like a really smart egg. Why hasn't he been given the Nobel yet? I mean, fuck, he knows what happens when we *die*. And he's not even dead yet. Not many people can say that. Sane people, anyway."

"Whatever. It means if you kick the bucket from smoking your ghost is gonna be smoking, too. Forever, D."

"And what would your apparition be doing? It'd be *whining*. An everlasting *whine*."

"I'm just trying to look out for my sis. I mean, you're only fourteen and you're smoking. It just worries me."

"Don't worry. I've been at it for a couple weeks now. I'm extremely relaxed. Extremely." Delphine then began coughing, like real wheezy coughing, bending her neck to the ground and almost keeling over, her face flushed red with a stalactite of spit hanging from her lip. "Extremely . . ."

Apart from all that the walk was like any other. The Populars at school always seemed to run past in herds, laughing those kinda laughs that you could be carted for. Burgess plodded along, catching up with his associate Sawyer to spout something about yesterday's new teen friendly TV show *Gaia Versus The World* and also about his sister, who was probably going to get cancer, he says to Sawyer.

"Yeah, I get that. But why is Gaia versus the world if Gaia *means* the world? It's versus itself?"

"What great force is not against itself, Sawyer?"

"So it's suicidal is what you're saying."

"Well, the planetary equivalent."

"Do you really think Del's gonna get cancer?"

"It just amazes me how *dumb* she is. She can quote The Tyger verbatim but she can't see what she's doing to herself."

"It does add a certain poise." Sawyer then began unawares to ogle at Burgess's sister about thirty steps in front.

"She's gonna smell like a Charles Dickens novel."

"Do you think I could ask her out today? If she's gonna die

soon."

"Again with this? It's like you've asked me a hundred times this week."

"Just interested."

"It's almost like this whole thing started at the same time she took up smoking." Burgess sunk his brow.

"..."

"She's a chimney, Sawyer. A Victorian chimney. You wanna kiss a Victorian chimney?"

Delphine herself made it to registration a little late due to her final cigarette turning into the penultimate. She was in a stall puffing out the little fenestration with her black Doc Martin boots resting duck footed on the toilet seat. One false slip and she'd meet the fishes. Now that she thought about it, mafioso gangsters probably found themselves in exactly these types of situations all the time. In medias res the door swung open, spilling out hallway noise. There was a knock on the stall door. She shouted *'Ocupado!'* but the knocker didn't seem to know Spanish and so kept on knocking. She resumed her endeavour, but the knocker continued to knock.

"*Vete a la mierda...*"

"Delphine? Is that you?" It was Ms. Blanco, her Spanish teacher. She could tell by the voice.

"Oh, Ms. Blanco. I was just trying to tell you I had some incense I was burning." Exhale. "My therapist says I have to breathe in incense whenever I'm beat."

"Incense? Smells like tobacco in there."

"It's tobacco scented incense. The smell of smoke reminds me of my grandfather. It's a very distinguished scent." At that moment there was a rectal release in the stall next to hers which didn't do much for her whole spiel.

"You will not fool me, Ms. Moon. That is *humo de cigarro.* And by the ways, you cannot say how are you in Spanish but you can say *that?"*

"Look, okay. I—"

"Can I have one?"

"Ey?"

"A cigarette," she says. "If you let me in then I'll spare the other teachers the news."

"You're yanking my melon? Surely?"

"No, Ms. Moon. No yanking. No melons."

"Umm. Okay. I guess you can have one." She unlocked the door and Ms. Blanco came in, optics protruding. "Jonesing, are we?"

"Very tired," she says. Delphine was still standing on the toilet. She handed the teacher a fresh Camel Blue and offered her lighter but Ms. Blanco had a Zippo ready. At this point, Del had already thrown her own bone in the toilet bowl and was just standing there on the seat while Blanco hunched up and began puffing, blocking any escape bar the little oblong window.

"Well. I should be shoving off."

"Hold on, let me get my flask out. Have you ever smoked with a cup of coffee? Bliss!"

"I'll remember to take a note of that. Can I get out now? My feet are starting to hurt."

"No coffee?" she says, revealing a flask. "Why, you simply must!" She then slapped Del's stomach in a way of friendly *vamos*, and Delphine went sinking, slipping down into the bowl boots first until she resembled a strange kind of mermaid, and Ms. Blanco, now eye to eye with her in the stall, grabbed her by the head and cried *Dios mío*.

hen his brother didn't come back with

the glue, Ori Moon had gone out to the Hub in the darkness of night to go get some himself, in order to fix up his time machine. Usually, Ori wasn't allowed to leave the house on his own even though he was eighteen years old and technically a man, but he went out to get the glue anyway, jumping out his bedroom window and abseiling down the lattice. The reason Mum had forbidden him to go all alfresco was because Ori Moon wasn't exactly the sharpest glue in the box and that he would probably get lost if he did leave, even though Mum promised it wasn't because he was a bad son. Everyone had told him such things, that he didn't have to feel bad about getting things wrong sometimes, because the paranormia was just something that happened to his head when the dinosaurs were around, and therefore not his fault he had a much harder fountain to climb than the rest, and but due to that he wasn't allowed to leave the house on his own and especially not at night. But it wasn't his fault, that he was dumb as a bag of Pogs, was the whole crucifix of the matter. Ori wasn't shirty about that stuff. He still felt emotions and he knew when he liked something. But his heart was in his skull and that's just the way it was. Ori never got shirty in fact, he never threw a phantom and he never got shirty at anybody, for anything. Why would he bother to get shirty at somebody, like Burgess forgetting the glue, when there were too many people shirty about something anyway, too many with steam coming out their ears? He didn't want to be like that, because how would he be able to listen to stuff like music, his favourite thing, through all that steam? The folks who had it come out their ears never usually listened to music because all they heard was the steam coming out. But even so, music wasn't just songs on the computer or noises from an instrument. It was, to him, also the sound of rain falling, and people sneezing in Irish flats, and other such things like that. Ori thinks about music all the time. He's pretty sure he's got melonmania. He notes the time on the machine (when it's working, that is) and listens for all of time. Sometimes he has music playing, but most of the time the music is in the street. People coughing up all sorts of stuff. Sometimes you hear someone say 'Thank God!' and you wonder what the people must have seen or heard to make them thank God, because no one really thanks God at all these days unless it's like a life and death situation or something, and so you wonder what must have happened out there in the street to make them thank God. It's all mystery. It's all music. Everything is a song.

So he went down to the Hub at like 4AM, the shop still open. It was a 24/7 gimmick they were employing. All perpetual and such. He looked in the big pixefied brochure, opening and closing it at random, as if the book was somehow having an epicurean fit. And so he was down at the Hub, where they teleported the products onto the Hub's counters once you'd found the code in the brochure and entered it and all, and then so the store was unmanned as normal and had those Port Slots in the counters where all your stuff manifolded for you. And it was so dark outside but real lit up inside and it felt like Ori was halfway in light and halfway in darkness. Like he was in a chiaroscuro scene. No one else around, though when he opened the door as he came in someone was coming out the same time holding a box, and they looked like they needed to sneeze but were holding it in.

After ages looking for the item in the book, and then finally typing in the code, Ori waited expectantly at Port Slot 4. He loved seeing the stuff come in. It was the coolest looking thing. You could see your reflection in the fuzzy arcaney portal, and then you were fuzzy too, and no one called you out for it and carted you away or locked you in a basement for saying the world was turning fuzzy. The smashproof glass that was over the Port Slots was meant so your hands didn't touch the portal when it was engaged, because that would cut off whatever you stuck in there and send it to an unknown destination in the galaxy. And so, the glass. When you'd paid and it was ready to take, the glass opened up this oval hatch thing and you could grab it. The only thing was Ori couldn't find his Hub card to pay. He looked around on the floor in case he'd dropped it, and happened to find someone else's instead. Turned out it was his friend's card. Jimmy One Hat. The glue was already transported and waiting in the glass. He decided to pay with Jimmy's card after looking in the brochure for so long, putting it in his pocket after so he could return it to Jimmy.

It was only a tube of glue and all. Still, Ori felt a bit gillty, so he left a quid and fifty pence next to the used Slot and scurried out, the time still 4AM, on the dot.

When he got to the Vox's house, he fixed his time machine before he went back to sleep, the flow of time now restored. But not in the usual way. He'd done this delightful thing and made it tick backwards. Anteclockwise. As he rested his weak body under the sheets and closed his sleepy orbs, he imagined almost to true belief that time was going backwards now, and he'd wake up yesterday, and know exactly what to do. But before he could conk, he remembered anxiously about the glue actually being too pound fifty, not one, and that he had only payed one pound fifty for it. It was already lightening outside and the birds had started chirpsing. Must've calibrated the time machine wrongly. But he was two tired to try and fix it. He got up and grabbed his other quid he'd kept next to his silver Buddha trinket and put on his jacket and shoes. He left the house, again from the lettice, and went back to the Hub to pay the final amount. And as he did so, walk up the road, a disembodied hand grabbed his right shoulder from behind and spun Ori all the ray wound.

"Excuse me, sir. We saw you in the shop earlier. Did you

think you were gonna get away with it?"

"Get away with what?"

"Paying coins at the Hub."

"What's wrong with coins?"

"Don't smartarse me. You know as well as I do coins are obsolete currency in the Hub. And you thought you'd give yourself a discount with someone else's card. Ey?"

"No, I didn't know coins were obscene. I swear, I didn't. I lost my card and I was just going back there now to pay the full amount, I wasn't trying to trick anybody."

"Don't push away from me," the policeman says, brandishing a pair of handcuffs and latching them onto his wrists.

"But I didn't steal the glue. I didn't steal it. Why are you taking me? Where am I going? I didn't know coins were obscene currency! I swear, I didn't. I wasn't being shirty. Burgess! They are resisting me! Burgess! Help! I didn't steal the glue, Burgess! I didn't steal the glue!"

After the fuzz had scooped him up, later on in the day, Old Florence Pipelli had come into the bedroom to give Ori his breakfast, still slightly inebriated from the night before, and beheld an unusually empty bed and above the curved wooden headrest his clock — albeit all now good and fixed — ticking the opposite way, and in that half drunk surreal moment, seeing his absence and the inverted clock above the curved wooden headrest in mad and mesmeric reversal, she almost thought he had finally done it. Achieved chronodromia. Went all transtemporal and such. Ruddy gone back in time.

VI

It was the kind of weather where you could feign a

tobacco habit. The resulting clouds somehow spectral and trivial at the same time. It was damn chapping. I mean, that shit had foregathered. Maybe when Christianity thought to associate Hell with heat and flames they were looking at it upside down. It was hellish, the cold. And so he feigned, passing the chains of time away in his new plastic abode, the old KX100. As a non smoker it was mildly entertaining and helped to ease the winter's entombment, but to his sister Del who chonged snouts like there was no next week, it wasn't much of a thrill to feign an exhale of pretend smoke, since upgrading to actual smoke had left her somewhat sceptical of any kind of amusement derived from the act. It made you contemplate your own mortality was the whole crux of the matter, she said, because of being addicted to it. In this way, it almost became a good thing. Not because you might die but because of their constant perennial cosmic whap of a reminder that eventually you will. Hourly. Or in some cases minutely. And it was sort of a good thing. A memento mori. He even knew a girl, Burgess did, that was purportedly in the know of some very valuable information of how a lad she knew had reputedly stumbled upon a girl who had a cousin who allegedly knew this dogwalker of a guy that was the brother of a woman whose therapist slash lover supposedly said that it was secondly, the smoking. Not even minutely. Forget hourly. It was a permanent cigarette in this person's mouth. They had a proclivity for smoking at night too, waking up every fifteen minutes for due process, the girl who found out the info said. Waking up and chain bunning these things like there was no tomorrow. Like, secondly. As in every few seconds. And how many seconds were in a whole day, he shuddered to think. And how many days in a decade, even. And decade millennium. And millennia teraannum.

Once he was extracted from the KX seventy two hours after he had first entered, Burgess's smartphone started vibrating an unsettling amount of times. There were death threats all over the shop, and he ended up stomping on his

43

phone out there on the street because the notifications wouldn't end. The people messaging him evidently weren't in a great mood about his little appearances on News Straight To Your Head the past few days. Folks didn't want their MPs taken away, that much was clear. It almost felt, aside from his father who had been uninstalled for several years, like he was the only one, the only one who hadn't copped the thing. The more they ruined actual existence the more they were used to alleviate that ruined existence. It was a way to get away without going away, to head into nature without heading into nature, to make an exodus all alone, to behold the invisible screen. It gave them the entire world, pixelated and pinned, and that allowed them to never be a part of it.

Walking back to his one bedroom flat in East Axberry — the tube of glue still stuck to the inside of his right chino pocket — Burgess passed a couple of kids on the street who were engaged in an aquatic MP related *folie à deux*. The girl was wearing a Gengar hat and the boy was wearing an oversized cardigan. They seemed to be swimming in the air, looking for something. Do you see it, says the girl, gargling. I see it, says the boy. They swam to the middle of the street together, the boy picking up a discarded can of Vimto and displaying it to the girl. Here, he says, gargling. This is the treasure we've been looking for. I see it, she says. What a find, she gargles. But what they didn't seem to find was the car coming right at them, barreling down like a juggernaut jalopy. They were completely oblivious. From the pavement Burgess could do nothing but look. He tried to shout to them but it was all in vain — they couldn't hear him. Time seemed to shift off grid for an instant and then rev back up and realign as the little swimmers met the grille and the windshield of the jalopy cracked apart amid a mighty metal howl. Contorted and entangled in the resulting shards and looming over the bludgeoned kids like a strange gargoyle, the driver hung there, his temples donned with the Frankensteinian bio pads of a newly obtained Mindphone installation. Burgess felt for his phone to call an ambulance but remembered that he had already stomped on it. The kids weren't dead but by the time they got to the hospital one of them was. The driver was playing a racing game on his MP it turned out, and so immersed in the game that he had forgotten he was in his car driving back from the Hub where he'd picked the thing up just half an hour before — the place where Ori thought teleportation was a thing but was merely a modern underground warehouse — mindlessly skipping the Orbo tutorial to go straight to the game. *This is so real*, he'd thought. *You can almost hear the pedestrians screaming at you.*

When he gets home, Burgess is still thinking about the little girl in the Gengar hat and the boy in the oversized cardigan. It was the boy that had died, it was later discovered. The way he didn't jump over there and push them aside like what you'd expect a good person to do.

He took a quick train to D's place up in West Croydon and made a mental note (this is not to be confused with the MP app 'MentalNote', mind) on the journey titled DUMB MISTAKES THAT YOU SHOULD KNOW ARE DUMB, getting to about twenty two mistakes in his old melon before docking at his sis's gaff unable to recall the traversal he'd just made, as if somnambulating once more, his movements slipshod from being in a phonebox for multiple days. As Shakespeare said, he's truly valiant that can wisely suffer. Yet upon his arrival he didn't even want to bother with telling his sister about all that stuff with the KX. It didn't exactly make him come off as a paragon of thought or anything. She might've known about it anyway, if she was watching News Straight To Your Head late at night and happened to see his old mug on her MP or something, spouting directly from the box, yet regardless if this was the case she made no comment on it. They were sitting in her bedroom and she started getting all papered up on a green ceramic bong. A Blu Tack'd NASA poster of the Hubble Ultra Deep Field with an image of the EHT M87 supermassive black hole superimposed in the centre hung above her goldy hair. The bookcase that lay opposite was so filled up it genuinely looked like it might collapse any minute under stellar death and pull them both in.

"Can I have some of that?" he says, sheepishly. She rolled her optics at the ceiling.

"Yeah, right."

"I'm serious. I know I've never done it. But maybe that's a reason to do it, you know? I was thinking about all the dumb mistakes I've made in my life. And then I started thinking about the things I haven't even *done*. The chances I never took."

"You sure took a chance with that shirt, though. Is that Granddad's?"

"Granddad never had a shirt. He wore vests all year round. Get your facts straight."

"I mean, if you were going to go for a drug I'd suggest a bit of the buddha. But this is different. You've never done anything. You've been freaking out about every little thing recently. Nice interview by the way."

"You saw it?"

"4AM's ma jam."

"Look, let me have some? Just a hit. Hell, anything you got. I wanna go crazy."

"Man, you're being a top melon right now. One toke and you'll turn into Raoul Duke. I'm not prepared to be your lawyer."

"Just give me something. A cigarette, even."

"No. *Definitely* not."

"But I'm so stressed."

"Then relax. Just be, B. Breathe in and breathe out. Be." She huffed on the bong. "B."

"D?"

"Yarp."

"You ever miss Dad?"

"Course I miss him."

"The Vox says we have to come home for Christmas dinner but he's not going to be there. Again."

"B. Dad isn't well. It's not like he's ignoring us. I just went and visited him the other day."

"Yeah. Well, at least we get to see Ori."

"Unless he actually makes that clock into a time machine and portals off into the future."

"I wouldn't discount it." Del then put the bong down next to her fishing boat ashtray and Burgess stood up to leave, eager to continue his mental tally of dumb mistakes that he should have known were dumb. "I need to get going. Don't get cancer, okay? And tell Shlomo I said hi."

"He's a cat, Burgess."

As he left the gaff, he still had this deep desire to go crazy somehow. Drugs seemed the most obvious way to do that, though perhaps just reeling off even more dumb mistakes that he should have known were dumb would have done it. He turned his shoulder and walked down the street, and in sheer belated wonderment he recalled the Constitutionally Loco that was still stuck in his right chino pocket. It couldn't have gone anywhere, that mother was glued. A queer choice of drug but a drug nonetheless. He'd just have to take these trousers off for a start. In the privacy of his own home. And then, for once in his miserable life, he'd finally take a bloody chance.

VII

For Jesus's supposed birthday, in her tried and true old sepia tone, Delphine agreed to come home for the first time in several years. She couldn't fight off the Vox Populi any longer, a nickname not unabsurdly bestowed by Del to her mother because she had a not too dissimilar sounding name (Florence 'Rox' Pipelli), and definitely not because it was an ironic insult. Definitely not.

Jesus wouldn't be there, the Vox said on the phone, evidently trying to lure her in. No Jesus. But Florence Pipelli used to think Jesus was white, so what did she know if Jesus would be there or not. Wasn't the point that he was everywhere, if he was anywhere? How could he not be there, as he was every erstwhile Xmas? Did she simply not invite him this time? Was he tied up in the cellar and would therefore be no trouble? She landed on: "What did you do with Jesus, Vox? Doesn't eternally mean just that? It's not pick & mix. You either believe he's here or you don't. I don't and I'm getting on just fine."

"..."

"If he *was* everywhere, he has to *still* be everywhere, right? But see, only nothing is everywhere. Big nothing, all around, Ma. Container of infinity. Bound not by space or dimension. A duffel full of nada. A big old bag of zilch."

"I fucked him."

"What?"

"Jesus."

"You fucked Jesus?"

"It was a dream," she slurs. "But yeah, we had sex, and it was one of those dreams where you know it's a dream at the time of the dream." Lambrini dripped from her mouth. It was poor times since Florence bet nearly half a thousand monkeys (not literal monkeys of course) on an online gambling session whereupon Cristal champagne was involved and many shots of whiskey, some inside the champagne to make a whacker when felt needed, and of course lost all the monkeys and almost all her money was gone or something like that from the bet, lost to all damnation and the reason why cheap Lambrini had unspooled from her mouth and not like Cristal as per usual. How did she ever afford ludicrous bets and Cristal in the first place? It was the money from all the screenplays she wrote. A fact that she would no doubt wish to tell you ad mortem if she got half a goddamn chance.

"Lucid dream."

"Yeah, that's it." A really rather disgusting belch came from the Vox's mouth.

"Jesus Christ."

"That's the guy."

"No. I mean *Jesus Christ*, Mum. So that's why he's not coming then. You're guilty or something."

"He agreed to skip town for a week."

"How was he, anyway?" she asked, already wincing at her own question.

"Best shag of my life."

"Go Jesus."

"Don't ever tell your father this, eh Delphine?"

"Believe me, Vox, I'm not telling anyone this."

And that was just on the *mindphone*. She still had to ambulate to the dreaded place and deal with this all over again face to face on JC's supposed birthday, with Dad and Ori not even in attendance, again most likely having to endure her mother's monologic declamations on her latest hit screenplay, nodding back in her trademark sepulchral sepia tone, a manuscript which she (Florence) would no doubt have proudly written drunk and edited drunk too and which was bound to sell not despite it being commercial balls but because of it. It didn't matter anyway, the grammar, her mother would say, because she had that good editor who would just fix it up for her (the editor that liked to bone her while Dad was off being carted). Again she and Burgess would hear, like a tipper lorry unloading a heap of sonic shit, of the awards potentially awarded, the nominations that were guaranteed, the *work* she had put in to write the thing. All of it another distended rotation of the Moon family. Same old shit. Same old Moons.

When old JC's day actually came, Delphine considered ducking out. Ducking out hard. But she had made one fatal error. She'd already shown up. At the table and everything. Out in the haze of the garden, entangled in the moonlight, streetlights beyond flickered against thick oak trees. What also emerged if you happened to be aware of it were near monolithic shadows across the concrete of the road that warped and even seemed to breathe, making nearby parked cars cast bouncing silhouettic twins and assembling phantoms out of light. From inside the window, Florence is yakking up rum and strawberries into the kitchen sink. Hitting the taps to wash it all away afterwards, she wiped clean wet hands on her wopsed head of hair and staggered back to the kitchen table. Burgess briefly mentioned something to her as they ate their turkey about being trapped in a box a week back, looking unusually sunken eyed. The Vox simply said what a charming story it was and patted him on the head, as if he was still a kid or something. There was no audible hum of any MPs in use at the table. Florence had sort of forbidden it this Xmas. She said it was because those things hindered actual conversation but the real reason of which Delphine all too presently suspected was that it just reminded her too much of Elbert. Sitting despondently at the table, Delphine looked around in that way people look around when they don't actually want to look at anything. To cut a long story short, her own damn mum was begging her not to go for a post prandial smoke and grabbing her arms and sort of locking in on them like a fleshy vice to stop her from leaving the table, and maybe the house too, and pleading to not do it and just use the patches, so she ended up shoving a couple of transdermals over her own eyelids and spasming next to the broccoli. The fleshy vice relented. It was like a sad tableau or something, orchestrated by an equally sad being. Everyone looked real somber. Staring at their plates. It wasn't really about the smoking. Or the patches on Del's eyes. It wasn't even really about Dad's absence either, something they had sort of come to expect when returning home for Xmas (seldom though they did). It was Ori's absence that got them. No one'd seen him in two days, the Vox said. Del was pretty sure there was a tear coming out her mother's eye, an eye veined with red webs. From all the booze.

VIII

It was at Axberry Wells Therapy Centre a few days later where Delphine Moon related what would eventually be coined the 'Iris Incident' to a one Madison Glab — a cylinder headed psychiatrist who'd been assigned to help her with her smoking, which in all fairness was getting out of control.

"I see. Both eyes?"

"Both eyes."

"And then you went and had a cigarette after, despite the superfluous levels of nicotine in the blood."

"Every time I don't get to have a cigarette I want to kill everyone and then myself. And especially when the Vox tells me I can't, when I'm a fully grown woman. I was *going* to tell her about the job interview I had for this spa resort up in

Mupfield the other day, you know, throw her a bone, 'cause it went real well. But I couldn't exactly mention it, after the whole incident."

"The Vox?"

"The Vox being Mum's nickname. Not like aural hallucinations or anything."

"I have a sense you don't like going there for Christmas."

"If I did like going there for Christmas, do you think I would have needed to nicotine patch my irises? Anyway, this talk re the Vox isn't helping I don't think. Can we go back to the guided meditation? You know, I'm here for the smoking. That's it."

"If that's what you want."

"What I want is to not be a hot mess. Actually, do you mind if I go for a smoke break? I'll be back in four minutes."

"Do you really think that's the best idea? I suppose, if you must."

"What kind of crap is that? It's that easy?"

"I can't stop you." She raised a pad of paper. "But maybe you can go after this. On the pad here is a cigarette. Now, here's a picture of that cigarette being smoked by a dead jellyfish. Anything come to mind? No wrong answers, Del."

"The murder weapon?"

"Try again."

"But you just said no wrong answers."

"I just mean carry on. What comes to mind?" Delphine leered at the photo.

"Death incarnate."

"And how does it make you feel, looking at this?"

"I told you. Death incarnate."

"Then why smoke?"

"Why take a shit, doc? Because you need a shit. A real Boris Johnson."

"Do you need the loo?"

"My brother says that you know, he calls a number two a Boris Johnson."

"Please, if you need to use the facilities."

"I need professional help. I've been at it as long as Tory rule. And it's just as poisonous. Just as expensive. Just as dangerous. Just as toxic. People avoid you, too. There's a lingering miasma. Sour taste in the mouth. Flammable." Glab remained quiet but only to allow Delphine to continue. "I can't smoke another cig. I really can't. You have to help me. Strap me down if necessary."

"Strapping down isn't really our policy here, Del." There was a pause that seemed to last for a millennium. The therapist's watch then let out a monotone alarm. It sounded tinny and weirdly otherworldly. Glab silenced it with a quick motion of her index and looked up, her opticaled eyes shrugging. There was no hum from any MP.

"Apologies. It's about time to stop now. Just try and use the patches as instructed next time, Delphine, dear." Glab led her out and opened the door for her exit, a free hand protruding to her glasses that had momentarily sunk half into her left cheek. "And remember what we talked about."

"A hot mess, doc."

It was a bizarre dismay that hit Delphine as she left a sandwich shop an hour after the meeting with the therapist. She saw her damn therapist. She was off the side of the graffitoed shop, meshed into the bricks, dourly burning a king size.

"Madison Effing Glab. What the hell. You're smoking? After all that shit you just said to me? I just bloody saw you. The dead jellyfish? The dead fucking *jellyfish*, Glab?"

"Look, I know this looks bad." Exhale.

"How can I trust you now is what I'm thinking."

"Do you really think this is strange? Something to remark upon? I'm off the clock. I'm having a cigarette. Sue me."

"Oh, I'll sue you alright. The accusation? Count the first: being a fucking basic bitch. See you in Hell, Glab."

So, what to do, now that her therapist couldn't be trusted. Now that everything was in disarray. Ah, she knows. A cigarette. A snout. A ruddy old gasper. Like good old Jesus did after he banged the Vox. She unsheathed her pack of Camel Blues and sparked a mother up. For some unquestionably disconcerting reason, the image of the postcoital Christ seemed to loiter around her head for a real long time. And he wasn't white. Because she wasn't a melon.

The smoke itself was not unlike a familiar companion. As if it could be called her perennial faux pas, an ever rotating mistake like the world in which she was encased.

Yet another smoke from a Camel left her almost infuriated. She was trying to quell something that couldn't be quelled. Her synapses felt ready to explode. Not knowing what else to do, she flicked the still lit cigarette right at herself and it bounced off her chin and practically torpedoed into her left jacket pocket, burning up her last remaining piece of clad that even had a pocket. A fallen hero. War is ugly. Especially with yourself.

She eventually got the Camel out after a few failed attempts and repaid it in kind with schizoid bootstomps, preserving — at least for now anyhow — the imponderable land of Delphine Moon.

Later, back at the flat, she noted grimly how an entire lighter's butane gas had been rinsed clean in just the space of a day. Couldn't help herself. The cigarettes had to stop. Her chest was starting to hurt. It was getting ridiculous. Glab was no help at all. Maybe that's why she was so tired all the time, now that she came to think of it. Tired wasn't even the word. It was more like she was keeping herself alive through necromancy. All that smoke had to be doing something. Or maybe it was just a conspiracy invented by the government. Why did she want one, when she just had one? Nothing to do, that's why. It was like a bulwark of empty space against her, taller than redwoods but no way to climb it. What remained was but thoughts of death, and chainsparking Camels and Amber Leaf rollups, the pouch of which showing the unsettling image of a baby stealing blems from the breast pocket of a decrepitly sour faced man busy at his work desk, the look on the guy's gulliver making the baby roar with laughter. A leonine laughter of death. Of carbon monoxide. And why the hell not.

distant belfry clanged. He was still at the

stone, the sooty granite now becoming both moonlit and twilit in the nascent Düsum dusk.

"Lyra?"

"..."

"I thought of this joke. Do you want to hear it?"

"..."

"If you're not in a mood to laugh then I won't."

"..."

"Maybe you can laugh at how bad it is. Yeah?"

"..."

"Why was the turtle sad at the library?"

"..."

"They didn't have any . . . hardbacks."

"..."

"I know. It's dumb."

"…"

"I learnt this word last night when I was reading my book. Elixir. I think me always coming here has something to do with its meaning somehow. Because whenever I'm here with you I always feel like I've drunk a strange brew. A good strange brew."

"…"

"Lyra?"

"…"

"…"

"…"

"Hey, Lyra?"

"Yeah?"

"!"

"Turn around, Elbie." In a state of panic, Elbert swivelled his body 180 degrees to find not that he had gone insane, nor the ghost of Lyra Castellanos behind him, but of something even more horrifying. It was the Wall. The Wall from school. Rick and Schmidt.

"Aww, he's talking to her grave. What's the problem, Elbie? No animate girls to talk to?"

"Get lost, Rick."

"You know she had a hairy lip, right?"

"Leave me alone."

"Or what?"

"Or I'll punch you in the head."

"Punch? Hell, that's a good joke, Elbie. Almost as funny as your fucking turtle quip."

"I'm not scared of you, Rick."

"Maybe you're scared of this though," he says, pushing on his henchman Schmidt's shoulders as if to tell him now was the time, Schmidt teasingly revealing to him something behind his kyphotic parka'd back. Before Elbert could even figure to duck, the open capped bottle eerily labelled with a big white skull was flung from Rick's henchman's hand straight into Elbert's face and it burned so much it burned it burned it burned it burned it burned it burned it burned so much it felt like he was going to die and sink into the earth like Hazel Kahn sunk into the earth as his starboard eyeball corroded away and became irisless — a state the Wall found humorous as it fell over beaming. He wailed an Aztec death pipe, the tears burning up before they even left his ducts. It was no dropped ice cream. And it wasn't a wolf. It was the hammerhead attack of sulfuric acid.

Rick and Schmidt cackled on down the hillock as they left,

ostensibly proud of what they had just done. Elbert had fallen to the ground on the mound of dirt in total spasmodic pain, clutching his pudgy face, which was a really bad idea because his hands also began to burn, hellishly, from the contact. He yelled to the blurred out stars, swirls of stelliforms, wailing like he'd never ever wailed before, and Lyra Castellanos — whose name and date on the tomb read now illegible and for all intents and purposes invisible, just like the little lady herself — once again made no reply.

He tumbled down the hillock instead of using his legs, gathering clumps of dirt and leaves along the way and even a snail who'd upped sticks to his back, somehow never getting crushed in the process (the snail). The whole right side of his head from crown to jowl was burning so fiercely it almost felt cold, like absolute zero on the Kelvin scale cold. There was an opaque black smudge appearing over his eastern eye's field of view as he rolled to ground level. He had a feeling he looked monsterish. The distortion didn't help him. He ran, then turned his six and ran back and really seemed to be lost just at the moment he stormed full pelt straight into his Ma's gaff's door's wood like a tiny little juggernaut, falling back on the patio floor, the smudge becoming one gargantuan smudge. His old compadre, the starless darkness, all around, leaking into every corner.

It was only a blink later when Elbert awakened to the sound
of a whistle. It wasn't an Aztec death whistle. It was the old
woman's whistle, the one in the red and gilt babushka, in a
bed across from his own, he realised now. He felt for the
bandages wrapped tautly around the starboard of his face
with hands that were also bandaged. The onyx hued smudge
was still there, tinged slightly with a pool of blood red that
danced around a mummified eye. He was sleepy.

"*Heeee.*"

"How'd I get here again?"

"*Heeee.*"

"Hey. It's you. So you didn't sink into the earth, then."

"*Heeee.*"

When Hazel Kahn had been wheeled away for her surgery,
the whistling leaked away up the corridor and into the
hospital's oblivion. A nurse called Johan removed his
bandages and took him to the sit down shower where he
was once again washing Elbert's face clear of all the acid that
had found its way on him from the scene up at the hillock,
with the shower head's water consistently poured all over

the burns for nearly thirty minutes straight before resterilisation and rebandaging, the pain numbed by some of that good old narcotic IV drip.

"My son," his ma said after they wheeled him back to his bay. "My poor, son."

"Ma?"

"I'm here, Elbert." She lay behind the smudge, on the starboard of the bed.

"I can't see you."

"I'm here."

"First the squid and now this. Ma? What's going to happen?"

"Well, you won't be able to use that eye over there for a start."

"But the doctor will fix it though, won't he? Ma?"

"..."

"That's what doctors do. They fix you."

"Some things can't be fixed, son."

"I'm scared, Ma."

"Don't be. I'm here."

"Can you sit over there? I can't see you like this." Alina shifted portside. He felt for his dome.

"Is that better?"

"…"

"You're going to be just fine, Elbert. Trust me." Alina held his hand. He thought about the bright side. The bright side of blindness.

"Will I still have to go to school? With Rick and Schmidt?"

"Not for a while. The doctor said you should stay at home and rest."

"Not for a while? Heck," he says. "I could get used to this." He knotted his fingers together and made a hammock for his head, elbows out. It was a weird pose to make for someone who'd just recently been attacked with acid, what with the mummified head and such. Alina laughed. She reached down for something in her bag.

"How about a game?"

"You brought the chessboard?"

"It's your favourite. How could I not."

"Sure. I'll play you, Ma." They set up the chessboard together which rested on Elbert's slidable tray. Nearby machines of unknown origin beeped and blurted. The onyx smudge was starting to hurt again. Alina moved her pawn.

"Did I ever tell you about the One Move Killer?" she says. "One move. That's it. One. Done. Dead."

"Ma, don't say one, will ya? I had two eyes, Ma. And now I

have one. So hearing one is kind of hard right now, Ma." He moved his pawn.

"They're going to give you a glass eye. Isn't that nice?" Alina moved her knight north.

"I'd rather just wear an eye patch."

"If that's what you want. But I've heard good things about these glass eyes."

"What's the chess move?"

"And it will be just as good as any *eye*."

"The move, Ma. Show me it?"

"Okay. But you must keep this secret. You take your king, and you —" Right then a doctor wandered in through the threshold and Alina went quiet. "I'll tell you later," she whispers behind her hand.

He was thinking about all that preapocalyptic time ago. Back in Germany, the dolphins, the woman in the reddy gold babushka. He was thinking real far back. Going deeper and deeper. Tunnelling. Right out of the ward and right out of existence. Lars Twiner, the guy who he seemed he could never get away from, nudged him on the shoulder in the cold game room with a hand that housed an unlit snout.

"Moon. Your move. Did you hear me? I said it's your

move."

"Move? Sorry, Lars. My mind was swimming." A young spindly patient who used to be a gravedigger shuffled past the room in borrowed clothes.

"We've been playing this game for a decade."

"Sorry, Lars. I'm just spacey . . . as little Devvy says," he says. "I was thinking back to when I was a child in Düsum."

"In the middle of our game?"

"This isn't the Olympiad, Lars."

"Look, you can't do that. We have a clear no think policy. You're the one who wrote the damn thing up."

"Lars, that was for tactical thinking. Not reminiscences."

"It's thinking all the same. I mean here we are having a nice game of chess when you start emitting *thoughts*? After everything we discussed. I mean, am I crazy here?"

"You're something, Twiner."

"You think they'll ever stop the rain sounds?" Lars fidgeted in his chair, looking all around his circumference.

"What's wrong with the rain sounds?"

"'Cause it ain't *raining*."

"It relaxes me deeply. It doesn't relax you deeply?"

"Makes me sick to my stomach. Drip fucking drop. It's abuse, Elbie."

"I was playing nice before, Lars, but I'll be damned if I sit here and let you talk smack about the rain. We got the fireplace noises taken last month, then the forest dawns went kaput. We can't lose the rain sounds."

"Oh, the effulgent *sounds*. The *sacred* sounds. How would we ever live *without* them? We would die! We w —"

"Checkmate."

"Get tae fuck, checkmate. Seriously?"

X

T

he PM leans at a hermetically sealed wooden

podium, standing also on a peach crate hidden from audience view. The audience are those using MPs on all the environs of Blighty. This was the lay of the land. No one there with Ken Pearly in actual human presence. This was due to an unforeseen zoological occurrence that very morning, where an apparently distressed zookeeper nine to fiving for Mupfield Zoo had set free a whole bunch of fauna from their steel cages real early — like dumb o'clock early — directing each animal personally to the opened portcullis at the front of the zoo. The zookeeper had purportedly done this, set free the animals, not only because of newly founded discrepancies with the act of caging animals in of itself but also due to the fact they had just been fired the very afternoon before, and they had no idea why they had been given the boot, since, in the keeper's mind, they had done nothing wrong to justify their being sacked. They had studiously fed the animals, cleaned up all the waste and even helped out the trainee keepers without the ask of extra coin. They clocked quite morosely it was probably because of last week's semi announcement that they did not in fact like to be called 'He' — and that after five years of hiding they didn't feel like hiding it any longer. It was so bafflingly maddening to the keeper that *that* would be the reason for the boot, that after they drove home, they decided to return to the zoo under the guise of night to wreak some kind of revenge. They thought about purloining some faeces and somehow getting it in the owner's office, but that required having to endure the horrible stench, which after five years they had still not gotten used to, and so kind of panicked about in the predawn hours of the unlit zoo wondering how to actually get some revenge going. And then the bolt fell. They would unlock all the cages and watch from the boss's viewing room window after jimmying the door's lock with an illegally installed hacking app, watch every single animal exit the zoo. And that's just what they did, connecting their MP to the room's speakers as they blasted Mozart's *Ave Verum Corpus* slumped contentedly at the boss's desk chair looking not at all clandestine. These now free beings included but were not limited to: hippopotami, penguins, serpents, apes and black maned lions. For some reason the sloths opted to hang back, waving in slow mo to their contemporaries.

So it was for this reason that Mupfield, situated on the outskirts of South London, had today been ravished and bespangled with creatures of all kind, two by two as it were, stampeding and slithering all over the crossroads, causing such a damn kerfuffle that London practically had to be shut down entirely until the matter could be resolved. The keeper had fled the area entirely by this point, and was nowhere to be seen.

And thus it was for this very reason that Prime Minister Ken Pearly had been sealed in a bite proof box and forced to address his first speech as PM out on the steps of Number 10 to a real life human audience of zilch. He addresses his camera projected from his own software installed head, thanking the Queen and such for signing off on the whole shebang.

". . . And so I am here today to tell you all, apart from being your new Prime Minister, that if you are in the London area, you must please stay at home. This is due to the Mupfield Zoo's horrendous breakout, which I'm sure you're all perfectly aware of. And I wanted to say to my friends in the country, we will get this sorted. Just please, if you are in the area, you must stay in your homes. Do not go out and take pictures. We will get this sorted. Imagine, if you will, what would have happened today if Kelp and her cronies had got their constitutional cake. They would be petting the animals. They would say it was a great moment for animal rights. We will get this sorted. And I want to say a few more things re Labour if I may. You know, the radical Left are once again, even as of today, luring the public with their usual lies against me. It's totally unsubstantiated. Totally unsubstantiated. Totally demonstrably inexorably incorrigibly unsubstantiated. And another thing, I've never copulated with a badger. Not once. I've sho —" Pearly realised he was going off script from the neurally linked autocue in his head.

". . . Labour using such insidious means of aiming to thwart all the good that *our* Party has done. What have the socialists done? A deal with the devil, my friends. A demonic deal. An entirely completely plethorically utterly indelibly demonic deal, my friends." At that moment several thousands closed the window in their skull and found other means of entertainment. Hundreds of thousands of others drooled spit into their government issued bibs, entranced by his gesticulations, which were visually pleasing.

"We inherited a sordid system, my friends. And we've come a long way. An undeniably implacably gigantically inalienably behemothically abundantly Sisyphusically long way. No thanks to Labour."

Several viewers' dictionary apps crashed in a desperate attempt to understand just what the hell this guy was saying. Did he not know, some left leaners mused to their spouses, that their very own Party had been in power for over a decade now, and that therefore calling blame on the opposition was not just ill spirited but flat out barmy? Nevermind the adverbs. Even Pearly himself didn't really know what he was saying, unwilling to stray far from the prepared script, written up presumably by some savant toddler with a bag of magic mushrooms and way too much time on their hands. Pearly had been screened to talk much longer than he already had, but cut the thing short as he began to see a herd of chimpanzees knuckle dragging their way across the horizon. Of course he could not be hurt but still, a visual image of flung shit at the box would no doubt have caused some PR nightmare to ensue, so he bid adieu after one more insistence to please stay inside, at least for the day, and that, together with all his other promises, it would get sorted. The hermetic box was then towed away in the fauna infested tangerine noon and back inside Number 10, Pearly bowing to the quarantined city's silent applause. This was the lay of the land.

There even had to be established a new governmental department, namely the Department of Perambulation, whose hazy raison d'être was supposedly to get folks to literally get up and move around once in a while and remove themselves from their mummifications, since the invention of interneural devices like the Mindphone effectively meant all who purchased it had everything at the blink of a button, and therefore little need to stay in motion. It became too easy to be a slob. Most work was done online anyway, ever since the pandemic four years before, and so even the sticklers were becoming slobs. All lackadaisical. Enter the Department of Perambulation. Their official gambit was that they were aiming to get people moving about more, ambulate, though unbeknownst to most of the public this was just another way to create even more funds for the Conservative Party, and that they didn't really care one way or the other if people were getting enough exercise.

Their actual meetings — though meetings were rarely held — were mainly for discussion on tactics of political maneuvering and general avoidance, the Orwellian marketing of MP propaganda, and a few smear campaigns thrown in there for fun. Corruption wasn't an impediment or enemy for the DoP. It was their requirement. Hidden, redacted, by an ever growing need for ambulation. They even issued an advert that spouted from the sky showing people how to walk and use their forearms. And of course, the government issued bibs.

The minds behind the DoP had established a brand spanking newly built office up in North Mupfield, located just on the outer edges of the Capital. It was put in Mupfield to aid their camouflage, a few glue barmy skateboarders from the nearby skate gaff Contused Neil's hypothesised, looking at the building, wondering if vengeance was needed for building over the Event Horizon, Neil Mosh's infamous black paint skate bowl. I mean, he actually made that thing. With his own two hands. And the Department of Perambulation just erased it. They erased the Event Horizon. Neil was babbling to Flynn Pillsly on a shift that the DoP owed him a check for filling in the Event Horizon and not telling him about it. Remuneration, he said. Pillsly just smiled weirdly, betraying a kind of boredom around the very thought of a government body. Neither noticed the pride of lions outside.

"Why don't we just egg their head office or something?"

"Egg the seventeenth floor? The seventeenth floor, Flynn?"

"We'll get a catapult." Neil rolled his optics at this but no more than a split second later began scratching his chin in ever expanding wonder until he was holding his dome and making faint paroxysmal spasms of awe, as if this catapulting idea was like a Newtonian or perhaps even Einsteinian epiphany.

"Let's do it," he finally spouts, releasing his gulliver.

"Here, I'll check," Pills says, blinking. "Ooh, ersatz mahogany. Does ersatz mean super? Super mahogany?"

"..."

"Mosh?"

"Sorry, just looking for my wrench. I think it means it's fake wood."

"This one's only thirty five. Hmm. Next day delivery you say? God, I love not having to hold a phone in front of my face. Don't you, Moshy?"

"My MP broke. Went tits up. Need to get a new one."

"How do you break an MP?"

"Landed head first after doing a monster flip down some stairs. Started glitching."

"You sure like to break stuff don't you. First your legs. Then your will. And now your MP. A true pastime."

"Shit just breaks," he says, expanding a free left hand and fanning it round as if to say 'just look', the other fist wrenching a sunlit bolt. There was a tattoo on his arm of a dragon.

XI

Delphine arose with an unlit cigar in her chops.

She blinked thrice and her home screen appeared, spitting out the Cuban (or hell, might've even been a Korean, it was hard to decipher what happened that night) once she clocked how late she was. The interview went stellar, she didn't want to ruin that by being late on the first day. But Del wasn't the sort of person that ran after anything. She also wasn't a light sleeper. Quite the opposite in fact. All that Cuban slash Korean cigar smell went right up her beak the whole bloody night and it didn't wake her up an inch. You could — if you were so inclined — walk into her bedroom at nighttime while she's asleep and such, and put on some Schoenberg really fucking loud, and she'd be lying there conked out ad ruddy aeternum with no awareness at all and precisely zero shits given.

Gargling mouthwash, she shoved on garbs and entombed herself in floral deodorant in a matter of seconds, though it wasn't like she was rushing. She just did stuff real quick. In one fell swoop. It was her modus operandi I guess you could say. Yet she never looked like she was rushing was the whole interesting point. It looked like a very efficient dance, no extraneous movements. No backpedaling or entering rooms wondering what the hell's going on. She had mastered a sort of synchronicity, her lateness today notwithstanding. It was like there really was a bonafide way to do things, and that was doing them in one great dance. One mad motion. Through the slats of the shutters golden bars had striped the flat, making Delphine look zebraish as she teleported around. Her MP was usually turned off after the time of day had been checked, and only turned on again if she needed to once again check the time. She liked doing this because every time you did that, turned it on or off, the virtual assistant Orbo appeared and flew around with its fairy wings asking if you'd like to hear a joke, and then changing its mind saying it was a dumb joke before you could even agree to hear it. Though, sometimes it decided to tell the joke and it was always a different joke. Orbo looked a bit like that fairy in *Ocarina of Time* — a luminous sphere with wings. The noise it made was of LIGO apprehending a gravity wave in the fabric of spacetime from the spiralled collision of two black holes. It gave you a heads up on how to use the device, and you could choose what colour Orbo was. Her Orbo was chartreuse. But other than the delight of seeing it fly up to her face and hearing the high warped chirp, there wasn't much impetus for her to use the thing. The MP's social media apps were not used at all anymore, they were off putting to her, and, being one with very little desire for interneural porno or telepathy, the device was mainly turned on only for the very occasional mindbook or to check the time and see the old Orbster again — and, when feeling impish enough, to implement the filter that made the walls ripple with flowers. Hundreds and thousands of them. It was top to see, but it did tend to get weary after a few hours. The flowers. It was intense. And that was just flora. She didn't even wanna think about the black market filters. It's like those guys sold nightmares. Like nightmares were their *trade*.

With the aforementioned flowers all around, she left the flat and headed for the bus. When it finally arrived (late, again) she grabbed a seat to find sitting next to her a thirty year old man in a suit playing on a yellow Game Boy Color.

She couldn't help but lean in and watch, and was so engrossed by the game the man was playing that when her stop had been reached she almost forgot she had to get off the bus, yelping at the bus driver as she lunged for the exit.

Once she had made it off the vehicle, almost truncating her own melon as she left the bus's gliding door, Delphine schlepped the rest of the car park and craned her neck way high to see the building in which she was voluntarily incarcerating herself this chapping morning. But when she made it to reception, she found from the operator of the desk that she was not in fact late but early. Ten hours to be specific.

"You mean, I'm early? I thought it said 6AM."

"PM," blurts the receptionist, pen in mouth.

"What do I do for ten hours, then?"

"Why don't you use the facilities? I can give you a free day pass if you want."

"Spend all day in a spa resort? I think I'd go mad." The receptionist bit down on her pen like she was trying to vampirically suck the ink right out.

"Mad?" she says through the pen. "You're leaving a great first impression."

"Just give me the damn pass."

84

She made a beeline straight for the Hotel across from the Resort, thinking there might be a vacant room where she could sleep. What she really wanted to do was go sleep in the sauna, but she wasn't keen on waking up as a dried piece of fruit. There was this glassed corridor about three stories up which ran from the Resort to the Hotel, resembling a kind of aeroplane jetty, with several staff swerving elegantly around her as she kept true down the arterial. The glass was so sparkly clean it almost looked invisible. Birds above the jetty evidently knew the score and always flew just atop or just below, never managing to bash their bird brains against the treacherous glass, though it was pretty obvious they had a deathwish coming round here. It seemed like a real risky gamble, sort of like an extreme sport.

As she neared the end of the jetty, Del craned her head once again to see a goshawk shooting straight down like a little kamikaze, only to pull up just at the last minute, fanning its wings to monstrous proportions and darting off into the milky hue of the overworld. Surely there must have been some collisions, she mused, now entering the Hotel. Perhaps they had cleaners specifically hired for just that situation: to wipe away birds that had stuck to the glass. Maybe that's what she was hired for, come to think of it.

Once she left the jetty, the building opened up into a sort of maze of right angles with several black shirted waiters rushing by in all theoretically possible directions. She didn't really know where to go, ending up in the kitchen somehow, only to be growled at by the chef who was wielding a machete. She walked back out and asked a nearby waiter where the Hotel rooms were, the man kindly stopping to point at the burgundy stairs that winded up just port of the entrance. She went up the stairs and tried a few doors, but none would open. Though she had a pass from the receptionist, it was only a Resort pass and not a Hotel pass. She fondled knobs ad infinitum, to no avail. Keeping on down the hall, she eventually clocked a door that was ajar right at the end. As she got closer she saw it was a bathroom. Hesitantly she went in, locked herself in a stall, slumped down on the toilet all somnolent, and did not awaken for several hours. She had dreamt about the dive bombing goshawk, and it just kept on dive bombing. Not reaching anything.

hen Del finally woke up, there was a

loud knocking on the stall door. She pretended to flush and came out, trying to hide her yawns. The cleaner looked irate. She blinked three times and her home screen appeared once more, showing that the time was 5:30PM. She'd been in that stall for eight hours. She went back up the hall and down the stairs and into the jetty, seeing no evidence of squashed avians. Somehow, she was going to be just on time for her introductory session with the manager. She went back to the front desk and noted that the receptionist was still being all vampiric with her ballpoint pen. It was only a matter of time before that sucker blew.

"Did you enjoy your stay in the resort?" she says.

"Sure did. Thanks for the pass."

"Kate will be out in a minute to see you."

"Thanks. Hey, you might wanna watch that pen you're feasting on. Looks like it's gonna supernova."

"Uh huh."

When the manager finally came out, she shook Delphine's hand firmly and escorted her around the place to show what would need cleaning. The woman was very large and sort of waddled around, though she seemed to have a distinctive aura about her, something that was either good news or bad news. After Kate had shown her the ropes as briefly as she could, she stationed Del at the cleaning cupboard at the rear of the Resort to start hanging fresh robes for the guests. There was a very specific knot technique used to tie the robes, something which became easier to crack once she had got going. She also piled fresh towels next to the robes, enjoying their clean smell. She did this for a dozen or so minutes and was eventually roused by a couple people who had come into the little room. They seemed to be banging on about voodoo or something just as bizarre as they hurried for the rear door, opening it up and producing cigarettes from pockets. A cold wind that might as well have been absolute zero rushed inside. She remembered fondly of her how Dad used to say that when she was only little, that it was absolute zero on the old K scale and such, and she had adored it without even knowing what it meant.

Floating back to the surface of reality, she folded and stacked more white towels as the duo continued their chat. Apparently one of the cleaners had a thing for making voodoo dolls in her spare time, to which the man next to her had all but choked up laughing. The moon above them was a faded ancient orb.

"Those things actually work?" he says to her.

"Buck, did you or did you not fall out of bed last night?"

"Wait. Hold on. Ya made one of me? Ya made a flipping voodoo doll of me, Flint?"

"Did you or did you not fall out of bed last night?" she repeated.

"Okay. I fell out of bed. That was your doing then? Why me, though?"

"Don't flatter yourself, Buck. I've got one of everyone. Even me."

"Even ya?"

"Even me."

"What about the Road?"

"The Road was the first one I made. I like to wake up and grab her doll and make out like it's having a heart attack.

One day, Buck."

"Hey," Del interrupts. "Are you guys taking a smoke break?"

"No, we're grazing. Of course we are. See the sign," the guy says, pointing to the sign on the door.

"On smoko? What the hell does that mean?"

"It means we're on our break," says the girl. "Buck just likes to call it a smoko. He's from New Zealand. Now he's bloody got me saying it."

"Oh, right."

"You coming on smoko?" he says.

"Sure. I'll come on smoko. You know what, it is quite fun to say." She made for the door and stepped outside with them, taking out a Camel.

"So you're the new recruit, then?" the girl says.

"Sure am."

"Little bit of advice. Don't piss off the Road."

"I'm not ditching yet. I only just started."

"No. *The* Road."

"Oh, you mean Kate? The boss?"

"She gets demonic sometimes. Just don't tick her off."

"Got it. So what are your guys' names?"

"Flint. That's Buck."

"Delphine."

"Nice to have another smoker, Delphine."

"My lungs would disagree," she says.

"I'm guessing you didn't tell the Road ya smoked?"

"No, I thought it would ruin my chances. You don't think she'll mind, do you?"

"Who, me?" She turned on her six to find Kate Road, staring straight at her like a bull.

"Delphine, come with me."

"But —"

"Now. And you two can piss off back to work an' all." Buck and Flint waved goodbye.

When the Road had shown her into her office, her face was sourer than a pot of Toxic Waste. She was anxious, partly because she didn't get to finish the Camel, but mostly because of the woman's face, which was reddening by the yoctosecond.

"You told me in the interview that you didn't smoke. You specifically said you didn't. Why did you lie? What kinda nerve do you have, coming into my establishment and flat out *lying* to me?"

"Is there a law against smoking I wasn't aware of?"

"I didn't hire you so you could fucking slack off with those *two morons*." The woman then grabbed her chest, her head momentarily tilted down.

"I wasn't slacking off. I was just saying hi to my colleagues." The head went up and then slung down again. "I mean, I'd had a real long nap and I just needed to take the edge off."

"..."

"Kate?"

"..."

"Fine. Ignore me. Like I care about this goddamn job anyway."

"..."

"Are you, *okay?*" The woman's head was still slung down, the crown of her blond hair pointed straight at her, not saying anything. Then the arm that had clutched her chest slumped off and was dangling at the floor, and she was all canted in the chair not moving, her hazely eyes wide open. She heaved up one of the wrists and felt for a pulse. There was none. The Road was dead. Paved over.

XIII

He was thinking about the first time he started

seeing things. On a chunky cathode that was not turned on, nineteen year old Elbert Moon, whose wispy auburn hair had turned quasi labyrinthine from resting against the headrest of his Strandmon for too long, found himself viewing a filmette being played on the greenish gold screen of the TV. The TV that was not turned on.

He pulled on the eye patch and let it swing back, his brows lifting. The screen had somehow yielded a mysterious field from the perspective of a resident horse. It was the only one there. You could see its hooves, hazy though they were through the veritable smudge. You could see the grass and hear when the hooves made muddy divots in the ground. The horse was a dull silver colour like that of a nimbus cloud. The sky, curiously, not seen. It rarely even looked straight ahead, the horse. Most of the time it was looking down at its shadow and the U-shaped divots it made in the mud. Where the horse was going could not be determined.

Although strange like a dream, he noticed it was not. He could tell by this little trick he learnt in a book about lucid dreaming, which he performed on himself during the preternatural broadcast of an unexplained equine galloping up an infinite field on his unplugged TV set, that if he were to plug his nose and hold his breath, he would still be able to breathe if it *were* a dream, such that if he could *not* breathe through it, then it must de facto be a non dream, i.e. waking life. The true dream. The one you can't arise from. Maybe one day it will be different, he thought. Maybe one day we'll all wake up. You know, he's reflected on it a lot, and if he ever does die, wake up as it were and sink into the earth, he would very much like chiseled on his tombstone the simple words: HE USED TO BE ALIVE. Or: MAN, HELL, SHIT. THIS? SO *THIS* IS THE AFTERLIFE? Or: THIS WHOLE THING USED TO BE A LOT LOUDER. Or: THIS IS STELLAR. I'M DEAD IN EVERY WEATHER. A CONK FOREVERMORE. WHILE IT RAINS ON THOSE EXISTING, MY KISMET'S ONE BIG SNORE.

He wants to get his tombstone done early. Is that weird?

Unpinching his ruddled beak, he gasped for air like a man recently drowned. No dream. Elbert continued — half mystified sewn tight into his Strandmon — to watch (and hear) the horse on the television, its strides hypnotic arpeggios. As his lower limbs jutted around nervously on the floor, his left heel caught the fangs of the plug of the cathode whose cord had slivered a serpentine path around his feet. The screen, though swamp tinted, was clear as crystal hygienically speaking, but that could not be said for the rest of the apparatus which had been thoroughly ignored cleanwise. Dust had for some time now gathered behind and on top, resembling a sourly grey candy floss.

Whilst the vision was vivid, and never strayed from the television's boundaries, Elbert noticed that the TV screen's rubberish hue was still visible through it, as if the vision was quantum-mechanically both there and not. He cannonballed his eye away and then quickly back to the square every once in a while to see if it would still remain, and it did. He was not quite scared by what was happening. It was more a deep absorption at what was happening. The stuff of dreams, he thought to himself. Beyond nature. Yet the inability to breathe after blocking out all circulation proved it was not the stuff of dreams at all. That, for whatever reason, an unplugged cathode ray tube television had esoterically aired a programme of some random horse riding up a nondescript greensward, not even with a rider but simply by its old phantasmal self. Only this. Why might be a good question. He left his bedroom and went to the toilet down the hall to whiz and fix his labyrinth and, coming back in a few minutes later and slumping down in the empty Strandmon — passing the framed photograph on the coffee table of him and his father Jupp on a boat in the grey North Sea — the unplugged cathode had finally returned to its inert pictureless state and there was no evidence or sign of any equine related behaviour whatsoever. He was flummoxed, to tell you the truth. It was almost as flummoxing as the Man Dilemma of 1993. See, Elbert Moon was formerly Elbert Mann, a surname which had to be ditched faster than anything once he moved to the U.K. due to the social confusion of the repeated general use of 'man' as a greeting there. It got confusing in public sometimes, especially since the gruesome acid attack seven years before which had left him blind in the right eye. All hey man's and yeah man's and yo man's and oh man's were weirdly directed straight to him. Mann. Strangers on phone calls were talking to *him*. Since the new name, it's less hassle. I mean, who shouts

Moon?

For whatever reason, things like the 'horsellucination' began to happen to Elbert more frequently around this time. Horses were everywhere, festooning his head. He went to a doctor about the problem, and the doctor said the images were unusual but ultimately harmless and not something to fear, that they were due to his impaired sight in his one remaining eye and that it was most likely something called Charles Bonnet Syndrome, a mild condition that affected the blind, and that he wasn't going crazy. Probably.

XIV

The following day, a big cardboard box fell at the porch of Contused Neil's. He waited for the postman to leave before putting on the new MP. Once she had, the bio pads were slapped on immediately and after only a mere few seconds the nanodevice had booted up. And lo, there was light.

"Hi! I'm Orbo, the Mindphone Guardian! Welcome to the world of the MIND! Oh, sorry. I should explain. Welcome to the world of the Maximum Immersion Neural Device! I just like to shorten it to MIND. It's cool, right? This is your MIND. Look around in all directions, it's circumambient. Not too shabby. The MIND's a colourful thing, isn't it? Speaking of, would you like me to change my colour? I can do that. Orbo can be any hue in the spectrum! Wow, great choice. No, seriously. The other fairies are gonna eat this swag up. I look fly! And yes, I see the irony... Anyhow, need some help there? Would you like me to show you a tutorial on how to use the MIND? It's quite intuitive. Alright then! I also thought of this hilarious joke but I'll wait till after. Might have to work on it a bit more. It's not even that funny, really. Depends if you like badgers. As I was saying, follow the screen and calibrate your MP's extraocular cursor now. It's super duper useful to navigate your MIND, and you can use it to 'blink' any button you see. Blinking is the new clicking, simply blink while positioning your extraocular cursor. It couldn't be easier! No need to worry about automatic blinking either, we've got it covered! Finally, make sure you are aware of your surroundings at all times when using the MIND, it can get quite immersive in here. That's about it. Phew, I'm beat from explaining! How about I just let you explore? Simply blink/wink on the ORBO button if you ever need a heads up. There are no limits when it comes to the MIND. Anything is possible. Anyway, gotta split. Orbo's got a date with a sprite! Adios!"

He dug further into the big cardboard box. Inside was the mini catapult that had been ordered the day before along with the replacement MP. He'd almost forgotten it was coming to be honest. Scanning the instructional manual he quickly got to work, laying it all out on the floor. Once the contraption had been assembled Neil loaded up his mindphone again and sent a message to coworker Flynn Pillsly and also Brodsky and Jhoanne Medzo — fellow shop and CL glue devotees — to go throw, or catapult rather, a missile of eggs at the seventeenth floor of the new governmental building, the one that was responsible for Neil's bowl being lost to oblivion, and they all agreed sans further debate. Of course, this kind of adventure necessitated even more glue huffing. I mean, it'd be weird if they weren't on glue, Flynn thunk. Doing this sting and all. Plastic Happy Shopper bags were taken out of every conceivable pocket, and capaciously lined. Neil reminded them once again how not to let the coated stuff on the inside stick to their mouths when they inhaled, because it wouldn't come off and they'd have a carrier bag stuck to their face, maybe forever. They clinked their bags together, made various salutes as if to say to each other bon voyage, and huffed all the ruddy way to Blursville. Shortly after, or perhaps hours later, who could tell, they left the shop and got on their boards, skating together like a pack of steezy wolves. Then some actual hippos showed up, most of them kid hippos but a couple of them old and colossal. Again these were somehow not noticed. Might've been due to all the Constitutionally Loco solvent they honked at C.N.'s. The world was like one big blur when huffing that stuff. Pillsly, at this very moment completely blitzkrieged on the infamous fumes, was holding the fake burlap sack full of chicken eggs and following Neil's lead on their board. About fifty were in there, and Brodsky was holding the catapult and even that looked small in Brodsky's hands, which were distended and chunky, like sailors' hands. Medzo was trailing along doing little 180s in her wake, half a pair of headphones in her skull. She had one of those cigarette holder things that elongated her smokes dramatically and which she did because she said it reduced finger stains. Jhoanne liked to keep it hanging from her mouth at all times, even if there was no cigarette in the holder. It made her voice kinda chunky like Brodsky's sailor hands. Chunky and scarred. Leaving the phalanx momentarily, she drifted up to a blur on the street.

"Medzo! Stop flirting with that CSO."

"Not flirting. 'm imprecating!"

"Huh?"

"Huh?"

"You still got the eggs, Pills?"

"Sure enough and yes I do," Pills says, undulating the sack. The CSO seemed he couldn't even be bothered with whatever shenanigans lay ahead, and left them alone, wandering up the pavement. "Put them in the freezer last night. They're rock hard."

Tracers of moonlight hit like jutted lightning bolts as the phalanx wheeled north up Mupfield. There was a black cat sitting on a recycling bin staring at their bubbles as they rode past and Medzo gave its head a little stroke. The narcosis of the night was wrapped around their skulls. The stars were faint. A couple SkyScreen videos were playing, something unidentifiable. Brodsky did a double heelflip and somehow avoided an elderly man that had fallen over on the street by doing a boneless over him. They still stopped to help him up, though, after. As it turned out, he'd fallen down after being knocked over by a hulkish mugger who'd lifted his wallet. The old fella wasn't even that angry. He was creasing up about it in fact, since all that happened to be in the wallet were some prophylactics from 2004. No money. No cards. No photos. Just some twenty year old johnnies. Brodsky shook the fella's hand before they departed again and even he made a comment on the old sailor hands that Brodsky wielded. After what seemed a short time, or perhaps an aeonic time, who could tell, they arrived at the veritable building that lay bricked above the long gone ghost of the Event Horizon.

"Wait. Hold on a second. How hard did you say those eggs —" Mosh began before turning his neck to see all too belatedly that Pillsly had already launched a bunch of the arsenal and they were for all intents and purposes winged rocks flying daemonically through the Mupfield sky gliding the air like undead birds in a sprightly parabolic curve — eventually smashing full damn throttle into the fifteenth, sixteenth and seventeenth floor's north office fenestrations, causing Gerrard M. Spank, head of the Department of Perambulation, to perambulate himself under his desk at high speed thinking it might be a terrorist coup. Why weren't the grenades blowing up? etc.

"What the hell is that? Are we being attacked?" He was praying silently from under his African blackwood desk where no one could see. Peter Stein, the intern, had to duck and did it clumsily though still somehow managed to miss a catapulted cryogenically frozen undead bird to the face, unlike Spank, who got hit threefold in the gulliver.

"Who are they?" he says, wiping shell shards from his neck.

"They're on skateboards looks like," says Stein, inclined to the window. The birds had ceased, all fifty had been evacuated from Pillsly's burlap. Spank got up from under the desk.

"What a load of nonsense."

"I mean. It is a form of perambulation, Mr. Spank, sir. Skateboarding and whatnot. Good for the environment, too." The intern was clotted with sweat from looking at Spank's face. A hell of a thing to do.

"Pete, it's not about the fucking perambulation," says Felice Belt, junior minister for social media affairs. "I mean, fuck. How dense is your bread loaf?" Spank peered out the cracked glass window. He let out a sigh.

"Okay. Get a window man, Stein. Coffee to the gills. And how do we fuck the way out of this Berkson Report?" he bellows across the office. "I need a knockout or it's your balls. Real *and* metaphysical. Throw all your shit at me. See what sticks."

"Say no more, Spank," yaps the young Roland Reynard Mug, before chiming quietly to Belt on his left — "Please, God. Say no more."

XV

Sophia Flint stirred. Early afternoon but already darkening outside. It was like night and day'd been fighting it out, to see who would win once and for all. She turned to her desk where the voodoo dolls were placed, and as she got out of bed and turned on her lamp the cotton sheets tumbled away and Buck's doll fell out the bed, looking a bit worse for wear. She couldn't remember if it was there because she was trying to cast a hex on it or if she was trying to emit a love slash pure sex not gonna lie spell. Generally you needed both those things when dealing with a guy like Buck Da Luz. Lovable and yet loathable. You really tended to like him at the same time as hating him. It was quite something. Like night and day in a barroom brawl.

She had a shower even though work wasn't scheduled like normal. As it turned out, the new girl was the one who had actually put the old kibosh on the Road by pissing her off so damn much she had a fatal cardiac arrest, and so there was a day off for everybody while a new CEO was appointed. But Sophia couldn't discount the possibility that the death was her own handy work. I mean, she was shaking that doll like a goddamn salt shaker. And then that happens. To her it was not a question of whether the voodoo dolls worked but how much they worked. She clocked early on that you couldn't just weave a doll and then poke it with a bread knife and expect results. You had to really meditate on it. It was a skill like any other, and if you had enough skill, then you could do anything. Adorning the oval mirror on either side the dolls lay with their backs to the wall, limbs drooping and eyes silent buttons. She had about two dozen of them at this juncture, some hexed, some blessed. It was getting to be a kind of obsession. Less and less space on the desk. Other things like books and trinkets also took up space, everything seemed to be balancing on a single thread of hair. A copy of *The Aleph* by Jorge Luis Borges was next to a doll of her own kind. Little Flint, she called it. The book resembled its bed, which it lay in vertically. Sheets dappled with words. She loomed above her woven menagerie. To them, she was a giantess. A weird and wingless angel.

Despite the fact she thought herself fair game, fellow family members didn't have any corresponding dolls. It was just easier. Careful not to mix relatives into the whole thing, Flint decided well before the shtick even began to cease any and all production of aforementioned famalam. For one, judging them wouldn't feel nice. She would be playing God on her own family, and she didn't much like the thought of the responsibilities involved. It was just easier to not make them. But the one of herself, well that one seemed necessary. She would do to Little Flint things she hadn't even done to any of the others. Sophia was her own worst critic. She beat herself up a lot of the time. Predominantly over nothing. About how the vitiligo on her chin was horrible and weird even though it was only contained to a small section on her chin. About how dumb she thought she was even though she read two hundred pages of *Being And Nothingness* all the way through and didn't have a brain seizure. About how unimportant she felt even though the new era of the MP in which she was encased was debatably even more unimportant. Somewhat surprisingly, after the new girl Del came back from talking with the Road that day at the Spa, she revealed her father was the one who actually invented the MP. She added, though, that it wasn't her dad's intention to make it unimportant. It just ended up unimportant. No one ever needed tits in their skull. No one ever needed to filter themselves so they appeared fifteen years younger on MP calls. No one needed blink operated gambling. But none of that stuff was him anyway, Del said. Once he had made the old Promethean leap, unironically naming his device the 'Godhead', certain under-the-rose blueprints of his apotheosis were obtained almost half a decade later via a cryptographic hacking of his PC by a newly developing tech company and patented for their own end as the 'Mindphone', defying his ardent heavenbent wish that it never be made for public release, even though he had spent over six years on it. Initially, the guy had wanted to create a computer interface for the blind, internet and everything, after losing most of his sight as a teenager, she said. Making the distinction also that it would be something different to just regular old VR or a pair of smartglasses. That you could see it even if you had no optics to speak of. In the same way that blind people sometimes see things that aren't there, the Godhead operating system exploited this phenomenon to present uploaded quantum imaging directly from the mind itself, bypassing the optic nerves entirely. Further still, about two thirds of the way into his project of creation, he clocked that, for good or ill, the technology could probably be used for many other things, too, including but not limited to: phoneless calls, hyper photography and film, recorded perception, recorded memory, augmented artistry, neural gaming, three dimensional music, instantaneous immersive visits halfway round the cosmos, and even enabling sufferers of hallucinations to be able to *pick* and *choose* what hallucinations they wanted to see and which ones they did not — all this thanks to a neurally installed wireless transcranial nanochip distilled into the brain via bio pads placed on each of the temples that seeped into your skin and journeyed through the neural network to reconfigure the visual cortex into displaying any number of chosen projections at will. No surgery required. All you needed was the nanochip and the pads. Interneural augmentation of reality, Del'd mumbled. Allegedly, her dad had this thing about seeing a lot of horses when he was busy working on the thing. He used to complain about them, always showing up in the darkness. She said he didn't even particularly like horses, and here were all these horses. And so he hacked his head. Saw zebras instead. And he wound up in the psychiatric ward, she said. But it was those first encounters with the TV equine all those moons ago that became the catalyst for his future understanding of visual fields with regard to a non optical dynamic. Flint was proper fascinated. She had an MP, in a way it was kind of old news, but this shit 180'd her head. How peculiar it was that the MP ended up in practically every noggin in the country, when at the very same time the man responsible for its inception was locked up in a madhouse. She couldn't help but conclude that maybe that's where everyone was gonna end up. Where they were all headed. But if everyone ended up in the madhouse, what madhouse would there be.

Flint yawned, noting the cooling of her brain. She was very much enjoying her day off. Normally, during work, she couldn't even yawn once if the Road was nearby. It looked like you weren't doing anything. No one saw your brain cooling. They just thought you were a topshelf slacker. But surely even Michelangelo let out a few yawns while knocking up the Sistine Chapel.

Preparing coffee in the kitchen, she turned on her MP, blinking her way to the news app. Surreally, one video claimed there had been a zoo breakout the week before, herds of animals festooning the city of London and bejewelling nearby Mupfield and Axberry. The reporter maintained the government had tried to veil their private orders that these creatures be terminated instead of merely tranquilised, and it had ignited a storm within the parties of both port and starboard; the left claiming the decision to terminate was inhumane and that the animals could just have easily been tranquilised and taken back to the zoo, and the right claiming they had to be shot because of the level of immediate danger they posed to the public. For this reason there was dead fauna all over the shop. Some of them bagged. The starboard PM had a history of hunting foxes, and would probably hunt humans if he could, was the general portside consensus. In more esoteric news, a representative of The Twisted Buddhas — also known as the Sleep Awakening Cult of Kinship, or S.A.C.K., an organisation that utilised hypnic jerks to reach 'twisted buddhahood', and borne in the town some forty years ago — struck out with their own thoughts on the matter, saying that the animals should have just been left to go about their animalistic business and maybe they'd reach twisted buddhahood like them and everything would be fine. There were rumours circulating from the mindmedia (twisted in its own right) that a handful of the creatures may have evaded capture but no one could neither confirm nor deny this. Possible lemurs in the vicinity etc. Flint wondered how the hell she'd missed this news. It occurred to her grimly that the reason for her unknowing probably had to do with her sleep schedule. Due to the night shifts at Illumine, the daylight was hardly seen. She would awaken in the evening, get on the bus that liked to be late in the shadow of winter night, and by sunrise be all the way back in bed conked out next to her menagerie. She must've simply failed to see them. In that moment, Sophia wondered how many other things she might have missed in her crepuscular state. Perhaps God had already revealed itself, only to be seen by the daywalkers. And perhaps that was why people at dawn always said hello to each other and why people at night always kept their lid shut. Why morning had prayers, and night paranoia. She blinked once more, closing the window. It gave her a little jump when the phone started ringing a few seconds later. It gave out no noise, merely a ticklish cranial vibration. Etched across her line of sight the words NEW GIRL appeared. She turned her optics starboard and winked at the green button.

"Hey, it's Del. Remember me?"

"Oh, hey there, Del. What's crack-a-lacking?"

"Just wondering what time you're coming in tonight."

"Coming in?"

"Yeah. Like what time."

"There's no work today. Have you already forgotten about the Road?"

"That was yesterday. I'm talking about today."

"Yesterday? Wait. Hold on a minute," Flint says, gazing at the date on her MP. "I was fucking asleep the whole of yesterday? I missed the entire day!"

"You must have slept for like twenty hours or some shit. Kudos."

"I miss the sun. You ever miss the sun?"

"It's been showing up in my dreams. I always have this dream of the sun rising, since I started the job. And it gets to the top of the sky and just cracks, that sonofabitch *cracks*. And then I'm wondering where the hell the light's gone, you know?"

"Cracks?"

"Like a goddamn lightbulb."

"Blimey."

"..."

"..."

"Hey, Sophia?"

"Ya."

"Do you think it's my fault that the Road is dead?"

"Like are you responsible, you mean?"

"Yeah," she says, stolidly. Flint looked down at the frayed doll of her old boss, picking it up and fondling it with her hands.

"I wouldn't worry, Del. Shite happens."

XVI

Ori lay in a bunk that licked the ceiling. The

bunk below Ori's — empty. The sheets were grey and weren't very comfortable, and the mattress felt like an elephant. He yawned. He was pretty sure it had been a long time and yet still none of the guards had come to his quarters and spoken to him about it. How could he tell them his story if they weren't going to listen to it.

His head felt orbicular. Like it was two present. Two round. The Plutonic form of round. All spheroidal. It was anziety, is what it was. Ori had a really bad case of that stuff. Suddenly every little sensation was unendurably overwhelming, even though there were no sensations. His ticker almost seemed to glitch, his head filling up with something that could only be described as helium, there in the top bunk of the cell. It felt like you could just die at any minute. Any second. But you never did. In a way that was like a prayer and yet not a prayer, Ori liked to explain things to himself to calm the anziety, which had always been around but which was especially bad now that the bobbies had scooped him up. He tried to focus. For one thing the cell was on the second floor in a building that stank of nothing in particular in a town called Axberry in a prison called HMP Axberry in a country called England on a planet called Dirt in a solar system suspiciously called The Solar System in a galaxy of milk named after a chocolate bar in a universe of spacetime. He thinks about the iron bars and he thinks about the sink and he thinks about the alchemical toilet where you're meant to do a number too, the still empty bunk, the smell of cold concrete, the absence of colour, the undecorative nature of it all. The night before, enmeshed once again in a chiaroscuro scene, Ori had eavesdrooped on a conversation from two young prisoners banging on about how sometimes you can get radios if you're good. But Ori was being good and there was no radio for Ori. Nearby, a guard was making some sort of joke to his guard friend. They both chortled and it echoed all over the shop. The punchline was: 'And then her head fell off.' Ori waved to the guards but they didn't seem to notice. They had given him food but it didn't feel nice like the Vox cooking for you. It felt, lonely. To pass the time, not wanting to pity himself, he began playing some music in his melon. No MP. He just made it up from scratch. In his skull and such. The music was improvised and sloppy in places but it was better than nothing. He sunk into a nap on the lunarly high bunk and closed his orbs. Someone nearby coughed. Turned out it was a guard, doing a cough in the way people cough when they want something from you. How come sneezes weren't like that? Ori opened his eyes.

"Moon. Get out of bed. You have an interview."

"Am I getting a job here?"

"You're very funny, Mr. Moon."

"So things will be explained?"

"Things will be explained. Now, come on." The guard fiddled with some keys and unlocked the door, the bars laterally adjusted. "Don't go running," she says, gesturing to the dungeon on her belt.

After she had walked him to the basement they entered a little room. It had that big mirror on the wall that they have to spy on you from, and there were too chairs just like in the movies. Someone else, a man this time, sat down with him and finally explained that the reason Ori was arrested was because they thought he was a solvent addict, and that's no doubt why he didn't pay for it properly, because he was hooked on the stuff, the man said. The perfect crime, except Ori didn't have a glue addiction and was just trying to fix his time machine, but when he said that to the man he laughed and said Ori was a funny guy just like the guard did even though Ori wasn't making jokes.

"Do I get a phone call?"

"We're swamped right now. Might take a while."

"How long is a while?"

"Soon, kid."

Hours passed back in his cell. Soon like heck.

"When is soon?" he says all belatedly to the guard outside. "Do I not have a right to a phone call?"

"..."

"Please, my friend." At that, the guard seemed to drop herself.

"Do you have an MP installed?" she says.

"An MP? No, I don't. Is that a problem? I don't want to be a problem. I mean, I did nothing wrong but I still don't want to be all shirty about it. You took me under false presences but I forgive you, friend. I truly forgive you, and everyone, and . . ." Ori shed a drop. "You take us but deep down we are the same. We all have the heart, and it beats in every cage." The guard looked Ori in the orbs, then down to her boots.

"I guess we can get a spare one from the office," she says. "There's a whole load of them for staff. Just make sure you uninstall it right after and it should be fine." The guard spoke briefly to her colleague and she made Ori walk around again. He was taken past the other cells and the cellmates were looking at Ori. He gave a half clocked smile at them and waved his cuffs, disappearing slowly out of sight. A few minutes of waiting and the bobbies made good on their promise of a call, and Ori, now all interneurally geared up at the office block, wondered who in the world right now he should call. And he thought about it a lot, and decided the best route of action was to ring up Rupy Mala, because she was a polygon of beauty and Ori liked the sound of her voice.

XVII

Mac Lorentz sits at his desk underneath the

presence of the twenty three million quid sapphire swordfish curio on the west facing wine red wall. He's fondling his silvery white goatee and making various varicoloured jottings on MentalNote with his extraocular cursor. Despite the corpse being taken away more than forty eight hours ago, and the thorough sterilisation undertaken by the cleaner Hilton Dax notwithstanding, still there remained in the office the aroma of death. Diluted death but death nonetheless. Death Lite. No one at the Spa really knows how this guy was hired to be the new CEO of Illumine other than that the previous CEO Kate Road had supposedly got chummy with him a while back, under real clandestine circumstances. All redacted and such. His silvered head is balding and he's about the age of fifty yet looks more around thirty somehow. Tall and slender with a big ovoid dome, warm ivory complexion, the benzoic hair making him look almost mythic. He was handsome, he thought. Very handsome. Mac likes to do tai chi in the office and doesn't mind if people notice. He actually enjoys being seen, has a real penchant for it, and his office has a window whose whole reason for being there is just so people can see him do tai chi through it. The sapphire swordfish is horizontally mounted with the sword at starboard and the caudal fin at portside, about a foot and a half long and curved at the ends like a crescent moon. A moon bejeweled with blue.

He finished a note and then blinked a few times, saving his files on a report of work morale. He was especially sore today from having met everyone, but only corporeally so. To give it to old Mac Lorentz, he did truly make an effort to meet every single person on the payroll on the first day of his reign. And he pretty much did meet everyone. Even the cleaners. It was a good day. The only hiccup was getting everyone into the executive sauna for an old morale booster at the same time. It was winter, so it actually felt rather nice to be moonbound on Io. The only problem was the morale booster went on for so long the warping effect started becoming less pleasant for some of the staff. People suddenly clocked they were half naked in a sauna. All pearlescent and such. Or at least Delphine clocked it, and she was scopophobic at the best of times. Flint and Buck weren't there to make it seem fun or interesting, probably still on smoko. It was just a whole bunch of men, ogling at her towel. She decided to retaliate with absurdism.

"Damn. Nice elbows, Dax."

"Why, thank you. I grew them myself."

"Fucking hot, they are."

"As I was saying, did anyone manage to come up with a mantra? Hilton? Francesca?"

"I thought of one, Mac."

"Go on, Delphine. What's your mantra?"

"Benzodiazepine benzodiazepine

benzodiazepine benzodiazepine benzodiazepine benzodiazepine
benzodiazepine benzodiazepine benzodiazepine benzodiazepine
benzodiazepine benzodiazepine benzodiazepine benzodiazepine
benzodiazepine benzodiazepine benzodiazepine benzodiazepine
benzodiazepine benzodiazepine benzodiazepine benzodiazepine
benzodiazepine benzodiazepine benzodiazepine benzodiazepine
benzodiazepine benzodiazepine benzodiazepine benzodiazepine
benzodiazepine benzodiazepine benzodiazepine benzodiazepine
benzodiazepine benzodiazepine benzodiazepine benzodiazepine
benzodiazepine benzodiazepine benzodiazepine benzodiazepine
benzodiazepine benzodiazepine benzodiazepine benzodiazepine
benzodiazepine benzodiazepine benzodiazepine benzodiazepine
benzodiazepine benzodiazepine benzodiazepine benzodiazepine
benzodiazepine benzodiazepine benzodiazepine benzodiazepine
benzodiazepine benzodiazepine benzodiazepine benzodiazepine
benzodiazepine benzodiazepine benzodiazepine ..."

After everyone exited the sauna, Mac stayed behind to clean it for some indecipherable reason. Bending down and everything. I mean, he was the boss, and he was cleaning up the goddamn sweat. Delphine didn't get it. The guy even had the nerve to give them all the day off and a bonus of half a monkey cash to boot. The Road must have been rolling in her grave the way this guy was acting. Next thing he'd be telling them they weren't going on *enough* smokos. Still, couldn't complain.

Strolling past the maple reception desk stationed by the woman who liked to vampirically ingest ink — Delphine, Flint, Hilton and Buck stepped through the foyer and hastily grabbed their coats from the coatroom. They slumped out into the carpark and just stood there awhile. The air was chapping. Absolute bloody zero.

"Can't believe he gave us the day off," says Flint, leaning against a pole.

"I know, right?"

"So, what do we do now."

"The world is our lobster."

"I think you mean oyster, Da Luz."

"No, lobster's what I meant."

Back in the head office, Mac's sipping some black coffee and chatting to Jack Cain, one of his port hand advisors. He presented Lorentz some virtual message samples via their connected MP headsets, and Mac was invited to sample the designs and give some feedback for Cain.

"See, this one is probably a bit too much. I don't like the

music. It's meant to be ambient."

"Would you prefer no music? Because that would require we get rid of most of the aural messages."

"Well, we have to have the aural messages. Change the music to something less horrendous and I think we've got something here, Jack."

"Perfect, Mr. Lorentz. I'll follow up with the representative later today. The installations should be done by morning. Operation Io is officially a-go-go."

"Just think, Cain. A month from now Illumine will be a greater force than gravity itself."

"Turning the whole town into a spa resort. Ingenious, sir."

"Just the beginning, Cain. Just the beginning. Once we get to Moon and acquire the MC, we turn . . . Gaia herself."

"Why stop there, though?"

" . . . "

" . . . "

"What does that even *mean*?"

"Forget it."

"Damn right we're forgetting it. That was the most moronic thing you've ever said."

"You hired me for my out-of-the-box thinking, sir."

"Yeah, out the box. Not out the fucking galaxy cluster."

XVIII

There's this girl in Butterfly Ward called Kira

Mizuki that knocks on people's heads like their heads are doors. True story. She waits on the porch and looks into their windows wearing her black faux leather jacket and sparkly silver skirt, preparing her knuckles. It's not even a joke, she really seems to be serious when she does it, knocking on the old frontal bones. If folk don't run away or recoil from the intrusion, she assumes they've opened the door. Some folk don't open the door, and they do that for various reasons. Sometimes, you don't want to open the door. Someone knocks on the wood and you wish you never had a house. She gets that. Kira has been in Butterfly Ward for a few weeks, and is starting to appreciate that some people will never open the door for her. I mean, why would they? Would *you* open the door for a ghost? The doctors are split on the matter, some open and some don't. But hardly anyone ever knocks back, except Dr. Nish and this guy called Duke who seems to think it's a joke but isn't being shirty about it like the rest, except it's not a joke though, she's full blown serious. Still, it's nice to have someone knock back once in a while. Duke has long black dreadlocks and wears this tartan red tammie cap over the top, clad in a raggedy brown work jacket which he wears every day, even when it's summer. Duke's been here a while.

Butterfly Ward is one of three wards in the gaff. There's Saturn Ward, Pepsi Ward, and Butterfly Ward, where she's at. It's quite funny name for the joint since the Ancient Greek word for butterfly is psyche. Plus, a butterfly coil can look like the infinity sign if you squint hard enough, and butterflies are in your stomach when you like somebody, and but thing is when old Mizuki here likes someone it's her brain that's housing the butterflies, not her stomach region. There's butterflies in her brain. Moths in her mind. Mizuki wonders if they had madhouses in Ancient Greece. Perhaps they were filled with butterflies. Wings shoved into straitjackets. All lepidopterological.

Down a corridor, Duke's taking a nap on the wall. A lot of

the times he's not even in his crypt, he's out, hovering around, napping on walls and climbing the floor, warped by a drug induced psychotic episode that went AWOL to the point it became a permanent disorder. Something to do with a forgotten sheets of three hundred and fifty tabs of lysergic acid inside his sock that seeped into his skin one day en route to a music festival in the Welsh wilderness. He wakes up from the wall dreaming of the very night. Ends up chatting to Simone Noirel about it, about how things happen when you think about them. All you have to do is *think* about them. Then they happen. Simone Noirel's an anorexic Franco-Belgian girl who always has her arms crossed as if she's carrying herself around in a bag. The rain tracks are spooling round, and Simone keeps looking up to the veiled sky to spot where the drops are coming down from.

"In Ancient Greece they might have concluded it was of supernatural significance," Simone says. "Here you're just crazy."

"We could have been gods."

"Instead, mere dogs." Across the corridor, Medium Nigel is shushing himself even though he's not saying anything. He's not a medium or any such thing like that. Just medium sized.

"I do wonder what the etymological correlations of the words 'god' and 'dog' are, if any. You know, Duke?"

"My legs ache."

"You've been sleeping on the wall for five hours straight. What do you expect?"

"The wall is better than the bed. I don't know why but I don't need to know why. It's just better." He raised his fleece collar and readjusted the tilted tammie, his elbow jutting out towards Simone's face. Kira pretended to not have been listening and went by all casual, as if she was on an espionage mission. It seemed like a bad time to knock, being on the old espionage mission and such, so she shoved her hands in the pockets of her black faux leather jacket and kept them there. Medium Nigel was gone. Or at least his shushes were.

"Are they both man's best friend?" she says out of the blue.

"Ey?"

"The correlation. Of gods. And dogs. That they are both man's best friend."

"They are, are they?"

"A man who has a dog is a god. A man who has a god is a dog. And a god who has a dog is a man."

"Well, when you say it like that."

"What if *God's* a dog?"

"Fuck. You've changed my life there, Duke."

"The Lord's my friend, but I'm not its!" yelps Nigel, putting in his own twopence down the far end of the long and winding corridor. He could hear them somehow. Mizuki blinked. She was entombed behind the eyelids in a world of imponderable rainbows.

"Kira?" says a westward voice. It was the voice of one of the doctors, Dr. Nish. She waited for Kira to reply but Kira didn't want to have to scream through the door. Luckily Dr. Nish was one of the few who — knowing that the girl liked people to knock on the old cranium and vice versa — would always throw her a bone with a little perfunctory knock, and so raised her knuckles and had at it.

"Go for Mizuki."

"Can we talk? In my office?"

"Sure," she says, following the doctor. Faces fluttered past. There were so many faces. What were they doing here?

"I'm afraid," Dr. Nish says as she closes the door, "that there is something I need to inform you of. Now, please, don't think this was my idea, because it wasn't."

"Is it a lobotomy? I'm getting a lobotomy?"

"No, dear."

"Shit. *Autopsy?*"

"It's your skirt."

"My skirt? How do you give an autopsy to a skirt?"

"Kira, the skirt has been causing some problems, problems that you might not even be aware of."

"It's not that short if that's what you're getting at."

"It's not the length that is causing the problem. It's the sparkle."

"The sparkle?"

"Yes, the sparkle. The *gleam*. See, what do I have written down here. Oh yes. *'The reflection is so profound it appears to be inducing several acute visions in an alarmingly high percentage of the residents in proximity.'*

"What's wrong with acute visions?"

"Well, Kira, I know that you personally feel differently about this than some of the other patients. But we've had several people telling us it's negatively affecting their stay."

"You want me to stop wearing the skirt? Because it's sparkly?"

"You're free to wear what you want, Kira. As long as it isn't *hallucination* inducing."

"I never read that clause. It's the only one I've got."

"There's one or two in the lost and found you could

borrow. Look, if it was up to me, I wouldn't be asking this of you. But it's outside my control, Kira. The sparkles have to go."

During this exchange, eighteen year old Dev Dwyer is lying on the azure carpet in the Chill Out Room of the newly furbished Pepsi Ward all the way down the other end of the hospital. The room has a conservatory that leads to a garden you're not allowed to go in. Dev's been sitting there on the carpet for what must be months. At least that's what he himself has deduced. All on his ones and holding his knees. There're books piled everywhere but when Dev gets ready to hunker down on one he realises the words inside have become hieroglyphical. The reason he hasn't been able to leave the room is quite devoid of any sense, yet in his mind it is the ironclad truth. Crack open his gulliver and what do you find? The sound of gunfire. The glass doesn't smash yet the audio is all too clear. It's gunfire. Vivid artillery. Been going on for months. Coming from all directions. You don't really get to see the news much in the ward, it's got Dev thinking there might be a war going on. In the Chill Out Room of Pepsi Ward. The shells don't hit you but you can hear them hitting you. They don't pierce the brain but you are dead all the same. He's yelling for help all over the shop but to no avail, it's all drowned out by the rain track. It's almost like something had got hold of his body and wouldn't relinquish its grip. A kind of energy. A kind of hell. As he lay there on the azure carpet grabbing his knees and hearing the deafening artillery all about him, a lopsided silhouette bowled up on the cream white wall. It stood there inert, all canted and thorny edged, seeming to be looking right at him. With no eyes. Resting on a cane. This whole shtick lasted maybe a few weeks was the general consensus among him and his neurons. He kept looking at it because it wouldn't leave, even during lights out it remained incomprehensibly there. A few days later, the silhouette finally opted to renounce its inertia and began peeling itself away from the drywall, revealing in its place a figure donned in a charcoal black eye patch and a green quilted jacket.

"Hello?"

"God, help me! HELLLLLLP!"

"Everything alright in there?"

"When will it stop? Oh, god. Oh GOD."

"Dev? Is that you there on the floor?"

"Elbert? What're you *doing* here?"

"I was just going for my noon constitutional. You've been

in there a —"

"A few months, I know."

"I was going to say you've been in there all morning. But yes, mornings, months. All the same thing really."

"You should get on the floor, Elbert. I think there's tanks."

"Are you sure you're alright, lad?" Dev had his hands wrapped around his dome.

"Is there a war here, Elbert?"

"Yes. But it's not bullets. Here, how about I schlep you back to your crypt. Up we go, come on." He picked up the young man and slung him across his back, the cane momentarily stuffed in his pocket.

"Are we the last ones left, Elbert?"

"We sure are, Dev old boy. The last of the lot."

XIX

Burgess Joseph Moon is looking at the red and

blue stripe on his white sport sock while a woman opposite is asking him questions. She's asking them now. He can't seem to concentrate. His trousers ends are stuffed into his socks to beat the chill. It's not like he wants to be here, having a job interview for an MP shop. But no one else is hiring. The Vox's payments ended a while ago, and he's running out of money. In the old last chance saloon and that.

"I presume you're familiar with how the phone works, Mr. Moon?" The woman was wearing a dark magenta pantsuit with a pumpkin orange shirt. She looked about thirty something, black locks and diminutive blue optics. One side of her hair was all wopsed up, as if she had been recently taking a nap. But that's just a guesstimate.

"Dad told me, on a few occasions. How he did it. I mean, there's no doubt he dumbed it down for my sake, but yeah, I know how it works. For the most part."

"And you've got one yourself?"

"I do. I love it. Ask anyone, I love that thing. Hell, what's not to like? Interneural screens? Ruddy love that stuff."

"What model do you have?"

"You know. The new one."

"The 85J?"

"Exactly. The 85J."

"You seem to know your stuff."

"That I do, Janet. That I do."

"I'm glad. How about now . . . we do some role play? I'll be a customer that's just walked in, you be the attendant. Got it?"

"Got it."

"Hi, there. I'm Jackie. I'm looking for an NP?"

"It's MP. With an M."

"Is it a great tactic to correct the customer so bluntly?"

"Well, if what they need to know are the facts, those are the facts."

"MP. What does it do?"

"It does everything. Literally everything."

"Literally everything?"

"Literally everything. As in like everything. It's been scientifically proven to do all this cool stuff, like record your memories and augment your surroundings, but if you just want to go on the internet there's that, too. You don't even need eyes."

"Okay. Let's drown this kitten. I like the cut of your job, Burgess."

"I hate to do this, but it's jib."

"Huh?"

"It's cut of your jib. Not job."

"Are you correcting me, now?"

"Sorry. So you like the cut of my . . . You know, if you hire me, you've chosen a guy who loves mindphones. Straight up. This guy? Ey oh! Ruddy love them. Can't get enough of them."

"Are you a gamer? Or do you use it more for newscasts? Or art? What's your *go-to* when you wake up in the morning and switch on your MP?" God, he really did not like her.

"There's not a thing I don't go on. I watch Gordon Ramsey shout at bread . . . and I play crazy golf with teenagers from South Korea . . . and I like to end most days with a bit of pretending to be in a rainforest. And I go on like every site. All of them. Like literally every single one."

"Every single one?"

"Every single one."

" …"

" …"

"Okay," she says, dragging out the word. "It's been nearly fifteen minutes. I think we should wrap this up. You did good. Was really nice to meet you. I'll make sure you find out immediately in regards to the position here."

"Thank you." He shook her hand. "I look forward to hearing."

Man, how many lies was that?

He got back to the flat, sidestepping a local hedgehog on his way to the front door. It was weird, ever since he huffed that Constitutionally Loco stuff he felt different in the dome. Never again. Why did it make him immediately yak up? Did that happen to everyone the first time? Was that the frisson you were expected to enjoy? Never bloody again. He closed his bedroom door, and a small carrier bag happened to fall off his wooden shelf and float down. He picked it up and peered across at the tube on the coffee table. Hell, once more? And then never again?

He found himself lining the plastic bag. Was just about to honk it up when his trap phone started making a noise. It was Janet, from MP Mania. After trying his main number and failing — since he'd been a right melon and Godzilla'd his smartphone — they used his secondary digits. They were calling him to let him know that, after a lot of deliberating, he'd been picked for the job, and could he come in later today. It surprised him, he never thought he'd actually get the bugger. Especially since on the application form he'd written down his mobile numbers but not his MP number, and for crying out loud, it was an MP *shop*. He blarneyed his way in at best. Knocking out porker after porker. Was she mad, this woman? Scrunching the unused paraphernalia in his fist, he chucked the ball in the bin, thanking her for this great opportunity to not die. It was truly bizarre. If they hadn't called at that moment, he would have ended up honking that hyperglue a second time. For ruddy bloody sure.

An hour later and he was back in the store, doing his training. They placed him on the checkout, flanked on either side by tall receptacles containing dozens of varicoloured fairy plush toys. He turned around to ask the manager something but the guy'd vamoosed. He sat down on a lanky stool and made a roof with his digits. At least they had the heating on. He untucked his trouser ends from his socks and looked impatiently at an imaginary watch on his wrist, even though no one could see him doing it. Neurasthenia was kicking in. Not even an hour at the job and he'd already become disenfranchised with it. No one'd even come in. Inert and enervated, he stood up and went over to the starboard receptacle and picked up one of the plush toys. He looked at it in his hand. A fine way to indoctrinate the children of the future. The soft surface, the wings. It's sinister, really.

After he sat back down on the stool, some woman and a kid walked into the store. He feigned a smile and asked them if they needed anything. The woman didn't even say anything, she seemed preoccupied. The kid picked up a few Orbos from the box, throwing them back when she got bored.

"There's no rainbow one..."

"Just pick one, Harriet."

"But there's no *rainbow*."

"Look, Harriet. I'm getting you a bleeding mindphone.

Don't be so spoilt."

"Mister, is there a rainbow one?"

"Sorry kid. Don't think there is." The woman walked over to the MP displays. The girl was looking up at Burgess, staring straight through the barrels of his eyes. He leant over to her.

"Is your mum getting you an MP, then?"

"Yeah."

"Are you sure that's a good idea? How old are ya?"

"Six."

"Jesus."

"Huh?"

"Look, kid. I'm gonna give you a heads up. This phone will destroy your life. It'll make your melon rot. You won't fly. You'll be comatosed."

"I won't become a toast..."

"What are you two chinwagging about?" says the mum, one of the display models hitched under her pit.

"I was just telling her how much fun she's going to have on her mindphone. Isn't that right?"

"He said I'd be toast."

XX

Florence Beau Pipelli, known by friends as Rox, by

sons and daughters as the Vox Populi, by one old lover as the Jagged Rox, and by the deities themselves as just another nondescript dipsomaniac — arises on a mid January dawn and sits up on the fine wood double bed to immediately swig a shot of Irish whiskey and slap her own face. She didn't really want to drink until Ori was found, still she found it woke her up quite well, that and slapping the face right after, in the morning.

She loaded up her MP, shaking away some ads with her cranium. No gambling anymore. No more monkeys. Not even a pony. Instead, she began another mindophony call with the local nick to see if they'd found out any more info. They hadn't. Claimed they'd misheard at first, that there was quote 'a misunderstanding of sorts'. Then she finds, spitting out her toothbrush, that Ori had been detained for purloining a tube of Constitutionally Loco and was not actually missing. It made her want to quaff more whiskey but she quashed that notion for obvious reasons. They made their comments. It all seemed like a mad dream.

"I don't understand," she says. "Why would you detain him? And why didn't you tell me?"

"Madam, your son has a solvent abuse problem. That's why he stole it. You just have to accept that. Accept that he lost his way."

"He didn't lose his way, but you've lost your mind, constable. What's your badge number?"

"Madam."

"He's a pacifist. He's a diamond. Ori would never steal."

"The evidence points to the contrary. We've seen the footage, he went in there, got a tube of Constitutionally Loco, didn't pay for it with his own card, just picked one up from the ground, and bolted. Why would someone who wasn't a glue addict steal glue and nothing else?"

"It's not exactly a bank robbery. I'm not happy about this constable, I have a horrible fear this arrest has a racial motive to it."

"We are merely abiding by the law."

"You've arrested an innocent young man and you're going to explain yourself right now because I'm not having it."

"..."

"Eh? All quiet on the western front? Am I seriously being ignored by the police? You arrest my baby, who's never even hurt a bee, on a charge of theft. It's a tube of glue, constable."

"Do you think we can just steal things, then. If they're cheap enough."

"I don't accept that he did steal it, though. You don't know him, he just wouldn't do that. I'd bet a thousand monkeys on it I'm that sure. A thousand monkeys, constable."

"Primates or cash?"

"What. Obviously I mean cash."

"Well, not obviously."

"Don't try and sidetrack me. I know the government thumb you're under. Ken bloody Pearly and that."

"And I suspect you're a subscriber of Liza Kelp's way of thinking."

"People are going to know about this, constable. If Ori isn't out by the end of the day, people are going to know about this. People are going to know."

"If that's all, Madam." Then the guy just hung up. Florence

peered about her, lowering her head. She shut off the system and just sat there in the kitchen. It was all a sort of emptiness. The empty house. It felt like deep space. Except you couldn't see any planets, or stars. The empty cosmos. The empty dromos.

Waking from a mist of narcosis several hours later, head in a right shambles, she jutted skullfirst out of a dream she was having that consisted of her first acquaintance with Elbert. It's not as if she wanted to have the dream, the dream just came. It's not like she'd wanted to drink the bevvy to the bone, the bevvy to the bone just came. And it's not like she'd wanted the men in white coats to come and take him away either, the men in white coats just came. They don't actually wear white coats, the ones that come to cart you off. But it's just easier to say that they do rather than say the men in juniper jumpers and blue bootcut jeans have come to cart you off.

The bubbles were bigger in the dream than they had been in real life. Like bowling ball big. Even though the kid's hoop was a small one. She saw again how the man just stood there as the boy with the bubbles began aiming his hoop up at him and blowing translucent orbs in his general direction.

Florence, just getting out of her day's work as a cleaner for a local parish church — her cigarette morphing into a porcelain Zulu pipe and vice versa — was observing the situation from across the London square, seeing how the wind cradled the bubbles into an ebullient Vitruvian wave, spiralling and splattering on the young man's face, a face that bore an eye patch and a coffee brown iris. She was perhaps waiting for the guy to tell the kid to knock it off or something but the guy never told the kid to knock it off. They popped against the felt of the patch, on and on, endless orbs like the endless orbs of a fizzed up pint glass of cornershop perry or the endless orbs of interstellar space and subatomic particles or the endless orbs in psychiatric wards. Not that she's seen any orbs herself. But she imagines if one were to be all *non compos mentis*, there'd be some sort of orbs involved. Orbs are in everything. The eye is an orb, and the sun is an orb, and God is an orb, and the Earth is an orb, and even sex is an orb, and love an orb also, and the mind an orb also. Everything great becomes orblike. Orbish. Even death is an orb. Don't ask her to explain herself. She wouldn't know where to start. Right bloody shambles. Anyway, back to the dream. It was warm that day, and in the dream it felt just the same. The bubble boy eventually left, his trail of spheres bouncing along the top of the river.

"Hey," she says to the guy. "Don't mean to intrude but . . . why didn't you tell that kid to knock it off?"

"Kid?"

"The one blowing bubbles in your face."

"Bubbles? Wait, that wasn't a dog licking my face?" Florence chuckled.

"I couldn't help but notice your composure."

"Merely an outward appearance. I am Elbert," he says.

"Nice to meet you, Elbert. I'm Florence. What are you up to, then? Waiting for a ride?"

"I am meeting someone around here soon."

"Stellar. Is that a Russian accent I can hear by the way?"

"Perhaps, though I am German."

"Have you lived here long?"

"Oh no, I have just arrived. I got off the plane this morning, in fact. I've come to see my friend Herschel. We're working on a paper together. He's letting me stay with him until I get my own place."

"Wow. A paper? And you've come all the way from Germany?"

"Yes."

"So is this your first time in London, then? Man, you've

got a tonne of great stuff to see. The Tate. The Science Museum. Heck. Sorry. I didn't mean *see*, because of your . . . I'm sorry."

"I like art and science very much," he says, seeming to ignore her neuroticism. "Maybe we could all go to the museum together. I'm sure Herschel wouldn't mind." She gazed downwards spying his beige Velcro chukka boots and frayed purple corduroys, then tilted her dome to the white cane in his hand planted in the pavement like a flower crack. Like a root of the earth, or an inverse bolt of lightning. The sun above him — a spinning pound coin.

"Sure," she says after an elongated pause. "I'll come along. I can show you around. Not *show* you around . . . Sorry. I'm really not meaning to be insulting."

"There is no insult taken."

"I keep saying daft things, though."

"Well, I am all ears. As you say." And then, the bubble burst, and she woke up back in bed.

XXI

On a fancy IMAX in a ghostly lit private

auditorium of the local Mupfield Multiplex, a holographic array of a becardiganed Leonard Swan — founder and CEO of Mindphone Co. — materialises on the screen holding his Russian Blue, Raphael. He then proceeds to step towards the audience, protruding further and further until he's not even on the screen anymore. Greeting them face to face, the holograph fumbles through the crowd, cat in tow, shaking their hands, to then return to the centre stage where at one manic moment the holograph disintegrates and becomes the actual man, Leonard Swan, holding his actual cat, Raphael. The folk are freaking out, everyone's clapping their hands into stumps. All slack jawed. Leonard bows indulgently to them, leaping right into a monologue about Harry Houdini, of all things. Burgess, who had been required to attend under the order of MP Mania (also slack jawed) — is shuffling in his seat almost hoping for a fire. It had been nearly two hours of shameless adverts on the IMAX before the guy even showed up. Probably late from being locked in a fridge freezer at the bottom of the Allegheny. And then there was like seven whole minutes of clapping. That's not even an exaggeration. That's four hundred and twenty seconds.

"When Houdini attempted a live burial in California near the turn of the twentieth century," Swan echoes, "submerged six feet deep in the dirt without a casket and manacled to boot, he was said to have been seen coming out several minutes later with a single hand outstretched above the soil, to which his assistants, seeing that he had lost consciousness, grabbed his protruded hand and pulled him out of the ground. He later wrote of the stunt in his diary: "With my last reserve I fought through, more sand than air entering my nostrils. The sunlight came like a blinding blessing and my friends about the grave said that, chalky pale and wild-eyed as I was, I presented the perfect imitation of a dead man rising." Or so the tale goes. Perhaps the single greatest illusionist of our time, Houdini was obsessed with escapologic feats and defying the laws of nature without claiming supernatural ability. When we think of what he was trying to accomplish, that is to escape naturally, what is it exactly that he was trying to escape from, bar shackles, tanks, and duck cloth jackets? Was he seeking escape from the mundanity of life? Was he seeking escape in order to find something novel and new therein? Was he escaping himself? Or was he finding himself? Some of you may be thinking escape is the coward's way out. But I ask you now, are books the coward's way out? Is escape from death a cowardly thing? Is art? A hundred years after his daring feats, we have found new ways to escape as a society. We escape ill health, we escape our demons, we escape. Are we cowards? Are astronauts cowards for floating in space? Escaping the very planet? I tell you, my esteemed guests, that escape is not a retreat but an exploration unto itself. Thus I present to you the latest innovation of the Mindphone, the 85X." Clap clap clap clap clap clap clap clap clap clap clap clap clap clap clap clap clap clap clap clap clap clap clap clap clap clap clap clap clap clap clap clap clap clap clap clap clap clap clap clap clap clap clap clap clap clap clap clap clap clap clap clap clap clap clap clap clap clap clap clap clap clap clap clap clap clap clap clap clap clap clap clap. "Thank you. No, you're the best! So this is the kind of stuff that you can do with the 85X." Swan gestures to the big screen behind him. "With the same N.C. bio pad technology but now even more enhanced, the 85X is a glimpse into the future of neural innovation. When I invented the Mindphone all those years back, I asked myself these questions about escape, and wondered what the ultimate escape could potentially be. The apotheosis. Now with even more immersive capabilities, the 85X puts Houdini and his shackles to shame. Now . . . we can all be escapologists. We can escape into our exploration. We can escape to the furthest reaches of the solar system and beyond. We can escape, with a mind that knows no bounds. A mind, freed from shackles." Burgess pretends to clap along, not making any contact with his hands. It reminded him of school assembly, when everyone would sing the songs and he'd just pretend to sing. He swivelled his head to the back of the auditorium, looking for someone to roll his optics at, and noted the reporter Joy Merchant in her usual grey pantsuit and black horn rimmed glasses sitting down jotting stuff in the air with her finger. He made a little wave to her, and she returned the gesture in kind. That interview he'd done on News Straight To Your Head a couple weeks back was the last time he'd seen her, so it was a pleasant surprise. The keynote speech went on a spell longer, and after another half hour that consisted mostly of visuals on the big screen interspersed with tales of how Swan came to create the device's intricate components, questions were opened up to the audience, several stumps flung high in the air.

"Hi, Mr. Swan," says a man in the crowd. "I guess what I want to ask is, what's the actual difference between the 85J and the 85X? Is it worth getting the 85X if I've just recently bought the 85J?"

"Thank you for your question, sir. There are indeed many reasons why you should get the latest model. Voxel resolution is three times the density than on the 85J. There is also a hefty increase in the RAM which will allow you to store even more memories than before. So to answer your query, it's the same device on the whole but with much greater capacity and immersion."

"Thanks."

"You, down there."

"Thank you, Leonard. I'm just wondering if there's a parental lock as there was on the previous model? I've heard that the X doesn't come with one."

"No need to worry, madam. There is indeed a parental lock just as there was on the 85J. We are very eager to ensure that adults as well as children are able to use the device safely, so rest assured. Can we have another question? Yes, you in the back."

"Hello there. What do you say, Mr. Swan, to the allegations that despite what you and your company claims, you did not actually invent the Mindphone?"

"I'm sorry?"

"Let me rephrase. Why are you falsely claiming that you are the inventor of the device? I have spoken with the actual inventor, and he tells me that you illegally acquired the prototype. I'm speaking of course about Elbert Moon, who never wanted the machine to be available to the public. And now that it is, I have to ask. Why? Why are you lying to these people?"

"Miss..."

"It's Joy."

"Well, Joy. You seem to have a very vivid mind." The crowd began chortling. "I don't know where you've found this information but there is a lot of deception in the press."

"I spoke to Elbert. You're lying through your fucking teeth."

"Are there any other questions?"

"And you have the nerve to lie to us about the lies." At this juncture the guests started booing. Swan looked irate. He raised his wrist to his face momentarily, then composed himself and resumed more questions from the audience. Burgess wanted to get up and leave right then because he knew she was right. He'd be well and truly fuego'd if he did, though. He turned around once more, hoping to give her a little salute of appreciation, and saw that the seat had been emptied. Joy was gone.

XXII

With the quid that Mac had bestowed upon them, the late night cleaning crew opted for a ride home in a limousine instead of bussing it. It was Buck's idea to hire one, and no one seemed to put up much of a fight. As they all piled in the back, the chauffeur nodded nondescriptly through the rearview mirror, seeming unconcerned that tonight's clientele were a pungent and sweaty lot of blue collars. Against the non reflective black tinted windows, rainstreams metastasised.

"So, where are you guys going?" he says.

"Oh, right. We have to be going somewhere."

"I can drive around in circles if you want."

"Let's go to the pub or something," says Buck. "Get royally turpentined."

"No need, Da Luz. There's bottles in that bucket down there. Yo, Mr. Are these drinks to take?"

"As long as you pay for them after, yes."

"Sweet."

"And have you decided where you're going yet?"

"Oh shit, yeah. Dax. What do you think?"

"Can you drive us around in tesseracts?"

"What?"

"You said you could drive us around in circles if we wanted. How about in tesseracts?"

"Sorry, pal. Don't have the fourth dimension on my satnav."

"You don't have the time?"

"What the hell is going on?"

"Too true, Flint. What the hell is a tesseract?"

"It's a hypercube."

"And a hypercube is?"

"Imagine a shape whose sides are cubes."

"Very helpful."

"Yo, this whisky is Scottish."

"Stop spilling it on my legs for Christ's sake, Del."

"Sorry, Flint."

"Look, guys. You'll have to get out if you're not going

anywhere."

"Oh, I know! Let's go to Flint's place."

"Why there?"

"So we can have a look at her voodoo dolls. What do you say, Soph?"

"I guess."

"And the address is?"

"It's up near Axberry. 39 Rose Avenue."

"Oh, yep. I know the place. Well, let's shoot off then, shall we?" And lo, there was locomotion.

"Gimme a lick of that scotch, Del?"

"Here ya go, Daxxy."

"Man," says Buck. "We're really in the wops here in't we?"

"Translation: ruddy nowhere."

"Nothing but trees."

"Nothing but nothing."

"How far is it?"

"Should be there in fifteen."

"Enough time for Del to projectile vomit."

"Are you calling me a lightweight?" She grabbed the bottle back from Hilton. "I'll drink ALL YOU under the table."

"Del, you're pointing at the car door."

"Jesus. These Scottish really know how to fuck up a liver."

"If you're gonna yak up, open the window before you do it."

"I'm not gonna yak up, Flint!"

"Buck, take it from her. She's gonna empty the sucker." At that moment, below the starry canopy of the elongated night, the limousine gave an unexpected sudden jerk and began to career off the right hand side of the road — the tyres screeching all banshee esque and shambolic before the vehicle curled in on itself ultimately halting in place and sitting lopsided and diagonal on the empty street. From the portside the figures responsible had come barreling down the long monochrome hill, seeming to be afloat holding plastic balloons. Turned out it was Mosh and co., the glue barmy skateheads, bombing full speed down the hill at whose base the vehicle had hulkily jerked, skidding off course as the unknown figures flew by spectral and unscathed, seemingly chuffed with the whole enterprise and raising their balloons in victory. As the car lay there inert, there came a vacuum of curious silence — inside and out — disturbed only by the gasping breaths and spat out scotch and sambuca.

"What the hell was that!"

"Is everyone alright back there?" The driver's head came

159

into view, owl spun and serious. "Is anyone hurt?"

"I'm okay," says Dax. "Just dizzy."

"We're fine," says Sophia, speaking for herself and Del who somehow hadn't managed to spill any booze. Buck was gripping his neck and moaning in incoherent Kiwi, hunched forward in his seat.

"Where the hell were you going, driver?"

"Had to veer. Some bloody skateboarders nearly hit us."

"Fuck," says Del. "I literally thought I was gonna die for a minute."

"From the collision or from liver failure?"

"All of the above, Flint. All of the above."

After they had resumed movement, becoming once again non diagonal, it wasn't long later that they reached Sophia's environs, old no. thirty nine — handing over various tentacles of twenties and tenners through the raised partition in one chaotic motion. Buck grabbed a few more bevvies from the bucket and they piled out the back doors, their breaths now illumined. Delphine was waved to a point where she attempted to shake the chauffeur's hand through the closed side door glass, precariously holding her bottle of sambuca in the other, commending him again and again for

160

not letting them die and such. The driver was patient and didn't seem irritated by her mania, and it was nice for someone not to be irritated by her mania. It made her feel less alone. Wasn't that what life was all about, she thunk. Becoming less alone. Finding kindred spirits. Finding. Becoming. Spirits.

When they got to the gaff, Flint propelled herself quicksmart into the shower. Da Luz, Moon and Dax were kicking their heels in the kitchenette drinking the rest of the booze, their eyes spiralling inward like accretion discs.

"Work tomorrow," says Del. Everyone sighed. "I'm gonna need a fucking year to sleep this shit off."

"More like a light year," burps Da Luz.

"Buck Rodgers over here. A light year is a measure of distance, not time."

"Chur, Daxxy. I'm sure that'll be helpful to know when I file my restraining order. I wanna be as far away from ya as photons from 2023."

"Gentlemen," Del interjects. "Can we get back to our work problem, i.e. going in for it."

"We'll chuck a sickie. Problem solved."

"Anyone need a shower?" says a still dripping Flint coming out of the bathroom. "Be warned, you might have to take one together. Not much hot water left."

"I'm not taking a shower with these melons."

"Why, is there a surface area issue?"

"What?"

"Your melons."

"Not *my* melons, Dax. *You* melons. You and Buck are the melons."

Deep after midnight, the foursome were all conked out bar Sophia, who stayed up to have one last smoke. Delphine had drifted off with her long fingers still coiled around a glass of sambuca, her lanky physique taking up a significant portion of the bedroom floor. Dax was next to Del, half in the bedroom and half in the living room, while Buck had managed his way into the bed with Flint. As she took her last drag, stumbling to stub the bone out in a yellow smiley ashtray next to the menagerie of dolls, she fell back into the bed and into a sorely needed sleep. A dream then came, and fire filled her lids. It was hard to tell how much time had passed, but as she lifted her lids she clocked she wasn't asleep. It was the voodoo dolls. They were all on fire.

She shoved Buck, screaming in his ear when he didn't arise, and when he lifted his own lids he soon clocked what had happened, and jumped off the bed and shook Del and Dax awake, and soon they clocked.

"Fire! Fucking fire!" Delphine, out of adrenaline fuelled instinct, threw what she thought was a glass of water at the blaze, the glass that she had fallen asleep with her fingers coiled around. She didn't remember that it was sambuca. Smoke and embers stretched about the room like shadows, the menagerie was engulfed.

"Shit."

"How, Flint? How!"

"My goddamn fag. I must've not deaded it!"

"Everyone go!"

"But my dolls! I can't leave them, Buck!"

"Flint, we gotta fucking go!" The three of them were already half out the flat door but hadn't left completely, waiting for Sophia who was still stuck to the bedroom floor like a statue, gazing at the flames. Little Flint was a goner. But Big Flint didn't have to be. Reluctantly, she turned to her friends and ran towards the open door, smoke filling her already smoke filled chest, and they bolted out the building together, their eyes unable to look away from the window that pulsed with Hadean hue. The menagerie was dead. Well and truly fuego'd. She couldn't help but wonder what on earth the hell it meant.

XXIII

The following night at Illumine, Francesca Ianni

was taking the brunt of Da Luz and co.'s frankly unmysterious absence, cursing into the doldrums of the toilet bowls in her native Italian, wishing she could be the one to bunk off and go on endless breaks. Her black hair was tied back yet nevertheless a couple nomad strands managed to escape, and one even went into the toilet bowl a couple inches, making her almost vomit. That being said, if there was one place you could yak up at work, then it was a toilet stall you were meant to be cleaning. As she lifted grime from the tiles, someone came in and alighted in the adjacent stall. She looked at the grime, hoping they weren't going to launch a missile. She'd just cleaned the sucker. Fortuitously, it was only a numero uno. They seemed to be chatting on the phone. She couldn't help but eavesdrop.

"No, seriously, Azlan. They've cut the fee by ninety five percent! I tell you, it's the best place I've ever been to, and I've been places. I'd actually live here full time if I could. The towels are softer than clouds. I've had at least four orgasms since I've been here. No one's the wiser. Trust me, you've got to get down here. I don't care what you're doing, just come. Illumine. That's the name. Yeah. I think so. Really? Jesus, Azlan. Okay, just put a pin in that for a second and come down. Drop everything and get in these fucking *towels*, Azlan. Yeah. You know, it's funny you say that. I was just thinking how good it would be if the whole town was a spa resort. Just spa resorts everywhere. No houses. Just spa resorts. The whole of town, nothing but spa resorts. Nothing but, Azlan. Am I? Hah. You'll change your tune once you get here. Alright. Text me when you're pulling in. Bye." She flushed and unlocked the door, whistling as she left. Ianni returned to the grime. Her world. Her grim, grimey world. Surely there was something more. But where was it?

Concurrently, Mac Lorentz was finishing off his daily tai chi in his office, once again underneath the sapphire swordfish objet d'art whose reflections of blue trickled through the viewing window, which, after the tai chi had been done, would return to being shut. No one could know what he was really up to. That is, not until they had been turned. But some good old tai chi. Who didn't like seeing that? Let's be honest, here. He was the most beautiful thing in the whole building. Even counting the swordfish. He pulled his last position, and shut the blinds. He wasn't nervous, still, he realised his plan was coming into fruition. The subliminal messages and chemically doused towels were extremely effective, it seemed nearly all of the guests who had arrived had been turned already. There was just one simple thing he had to do in order to ram this shit into fifth gear, and that was to invite a very esteemed guest to the Resort. A very esteemed guest indeed. And that was Mr. Kenneth John Pearly. He knew the PM from fox hunting years ago, it so happened, and they had been on affable terms, remaining in contact for the occasional engagement in various brutish behaviours. There was no way he would refuse a free visit. He'd give him the works. The whole damn treatment. Lorentz went giddy at the thought of it, having possibly the most powerful man in England in the palm of his hand. He never really liked the fucker anyway. He much preferred himself.

When Francesca finished doing the toilets, she went on to the showers. She grabbed the hose from a side closet and slung it by the first shower. As she did so, a towelled old man came walking by and lost his goddamn marbles.

"Oi!" he says. "That's a fucking hazard! Are you an idiot? Do you know how much my head is insured for? Millions! And you wanna crack it open with your bloody *death traps?*"

"You're a fucking hazard," she mumbles under her breath.

"What was that?"

"I'm sorry, sir. We need to get this hose out to clean the showers."

"Just be *aware*, for Christ's sake." He sauntered off, and she gave him two crooked fingers behind his shiny wrinkled back. Rich people are the worst. The worst. So, thinking about it, it was probably good that she'd never be one.

"Kenny boy. It's Lorentz. I'm good, my friend. I feel on top of the world. And you? Well, that's great. A whole turkey baster? Maybe you want to celebrate with a free visit to Illumine? Come on, now. You're not that busy. Being PM is a piece of piss, Pearly boy. Just never stop lying. That's it. Never stopping. Never once admitting you were wrong. Twisting every conceivable angle so the sparks avoid you and hit everyone else. Pitting people against each other so they don't have time to fight you. Now don't tell me you're the busy one. I won't have it. Is that so? Well, I'm glad you've come around. Why don't you come around not only figuratively but literally, too? Tonight would be better than tomorrow. Think about it. You've got that important conference tomorrow afternoon. Why not destress now? Before the big event? That's what I've been saying. Yes. Completely free. We can have cameras or we can not have cameras. Depends if you want to make this a PR thing. Yes, I agree. It could be good press. For both of us. By all accounts, my friend. It's all up to you. Well, are you sure? And you'll be here by the hour? Okay. Perfect. You've made the right decision, my friend. We've got a special floatation tank just installed this morning. Top of the line. It's got your name on it, Kenny old boy. Fully tailored experience. The whole shebang. Just for you. Yes. The dregs don't have a clue. It's just for you, Pearly. Just for you."

XXIV

Yulian Brodsky is up at dawn. Not exactly an

early bird. Rather a really, really late bird. Up all night huffing CL. It was strange, it felt like he'd been on the stuff for years, yet in actuality, unbeknownst to his funked up dome, only a dozen days had passed since Neil had first clocked them to it. What was the word. Anaemic? No. Aeonic. Felt like an aeonic time, on the old CL. But who could really tell? In a certain sense Outside of time, even Brodsky knew what he was doing to himself. He just didn't care. It was a breeze not to care when you were huffing. So the spiral goes, you usually care so little that you end up having unusually more, and then, perhaps, one day, you get to the end of the rutted road and before you even notice you've become someone else entirely, one who not only cares for nothing but one who will in fact never be able to care again. Ah. Who cares, anyway? It's dawn. The sun is a mountainous sliver, rising from the hallowed ground of the horizon. It's dawn. The birds have woken up and are tuning their instruments. It's dawn. It's dawn.

He stepped inside, stubbing his gasper into an empty plant pot. It was a houseshare sort of thing, but no one was ever home. He walked up the staircase and into his bedroom. How long was that? A month? A femtosecond? Who the bloody hell could tell. Yawning all over the shop, Yulian torpedoed into his bed, covers and all, and flicked on the TV. Too early to use an MP. It was dawn. Did he mention? So he flicked on the TV and all that, and that took maybe a bloody fortnight, no exaggeration, and BBC News happened to be on, with a red banner at the bottom showing what could only be described as indecipherable hieratic script. He focused on the audio; his ears weren't as distorted.

"While critics say the Town Resort Integration Programme of Mupfield — situated in Berkshire on the outer edges of our nation's Capital — is a precedent too bizarre to hold any serious long term office in the minds of this country's government, many people of the town are getting into the idea, with record numbers of admissions to the spa in the last week. In summation, this is what the

TRIP intends to accomplish — a systematic paradigm shift in the way we think about housing and relaxation. That is, constructing the largest series of spa resort and hotel complexes in the world, and placing it right in the town of Mupfield, England. As accommodation is torn down in order to make space for the spas, residents of the area will be asked to move out of their homes and relocate to the five star hotels just off the resort, and even put in work shifts in order to pay for the spa's luxurious facilities, if they don't currently have the cash. But as they've practically axed their admission fees, there's not much of a financial concern. It's a scheme that, backed by the Tory Cabinet and indeed the Prime Minister — and even Opposition Leader Liza Kelp — seems to have fought little friction in the area and in the country as a whole, with many public polls implying it would be beneficial for all parties involved to not make a U-turn on the initiative, including of course Illumine Spa, who are funding the vast programme. By melding housing with entertainment in one elegant move, and with the threats of social alienation and political disorder taut, many feel this is a step forward in communal organisation. And it all starts here, in Mupfield Town, the prototype for possible future expansions of the Illumine TRIP in other towns across the country. Either way you look at it, this is what the people of the town are crying out for. Let's hope in the next few weeks, as the complexes are raised, that they did not regret their decision. Rebbeca Warm, BBC News, Mupfield." At that juncture, a knock on the front door. He rolled himself off the bed and onto the carpet and just kept on rolling, past the bedroom door, across the landing and down the stairs in his navy blue robe.

"Yulian? You up?"

"..."

"Wanna go for a quick sesh?"

"Hold on, Moshy. Just let me roll up the stairs here."

"I got you a present. It's your birthday, right?"

"Really? You brought me a present?" He clambered up and opened the door. Mosh was there, holding up a skateboard.

"How dope is this? Pillsly did the artwork."

"Is that a cyclops wearing a monocle? This is real thoughtful, Neil."

"Come on. Let's go wear this fucker out."

"I'm coming. Just let me put on some clothes."

"True enough. You don't want that robe flapping in the wind. Some old lady might have a stroke." And lo, Brodsky rolled back up to his bedroom. Don't ask how.

He told Neil about the being Outside of time thing when he came back down. Neil said he wasn't just Outside of time, he was Outside of his skull. He'd left his dome and went to buy cigarettes and never came back. At this point in the game, Neil averred, old Brodsky wouldn't be able to tell a yard from a Planck length, let alone a minute from a morning. It's what the glue did. Threw your dome out the window. A one way flight to the exosphere. A real cranial checkout.

They skated about the street, doing slappys on the pavement. It was still dawn. Either that meant only a few minutes had passed, or else it was an entirely new day. Did it really matter, though? It was always now. Never not. Maybe time was dead, he thunk. An arrow stuck inside the forehead. A frozen ocean. Without motion. A wave at once suspended.

Conversing now only through telepathy, the pair of them headed to Dosborough Park, their regular haunt since the Event Horizon's demise. No one else was around, and for that reason it evoked a postapocalyptic sensibility to the place. Or perhaps preapocalyptic. Who the ruddy hell could tell.

"CSO at twelve o'clock."

"Great, now they're up at dawn? When will these guys stop?"

"Won't rest until every fag butt is behind bins. Here, turn in right here." They alighted at the back of some broken down kebab shop, getting out their lined polythene bags. Brodsky eyed his old sailor hands under the moonlight. They seemed to be becoming less sailory.

"We really need to stop this shit."

"Just not today."

"Exactly, Brodsky. Just not today."

"Isn't it always today, though?"

"Huh?"

"Isn't today always . . . today?"

"Brodsky, mate. You haven't even honked yet."

"No, I've been honking all night. Haven't stopped." Honk.

"Haven't stopped?" Honk.

"Haven't stopped." Honk. And such a big honk it was, so voluminous and vast, that his little Russian pumper simply couldn't keep up this time. He collapsed on the asphalt, his ribs rattling from a heart gone schizoid, until all function inevitably ceased, and there was no beat, and it was still dawn.

XXV

Pluviophiles at Dosborough Independent

Psychiatric House Unit (abbreviated by folk in the know to DIPHU, a Dimasa word meaning literally 'white water') are somewhat torn on the matter of the audio tracks that perpetually play throughout the House. While they have a generally relaxing quality to them, there is of course no feeling of the rain actually touching you, and that's a big part of being a pluviophile. The haptics. Not just hearing it but feeling it, too. It's mainly why people who are suffering extreme inner turmoil tend to walk around in the rain during a storm. So they can feel something. At Dosborough House, however, there are of course no such liberties of feeling. Like the patients themselves, the sounds remain merely disembodied. Incorporeal. Doctored. Falling in the skull but not on the skin. And so they stand there, circling their crypts, staring at ceilings, waiting to feel something.

After the morning med call, Elbert was reminded by the mirthful nurse Ohmar that he was due to have a meeting with one of the inhouse doctors at 1PM. Elbert joked that he'd check his schedule and if the window happened to be free then yes he would be there. The nurse thought this quite amusing, and was still chuckling about it as Elbert left the dispensary. He guessed there wasn't much to laugh about here, and so it was nice in a way. They do say it's the best medicine. Along with quetiapine and clozapine.

He lay down on the rigid bed and took a well deserved nap still wearing his quilted jacket. Was just about to nod off when Twiner materialised, his melon poking through the window of Elbert's crypt door. He couldn't shake this guy. Being incarcerated wasn't slowing him down at all.

"What is it, Lars?"

"Can I come in?"

"How could I refuse." Opening the weighty door and spooling in from the corridor, Twiner had in tow his old walnut chessboard, the one that doubled up as a little suitcase for itself, and as he came through the threshold the case came apart at the hinges and all the pieces fell on the linoleum floor, making a queerly satisfying sound.

"Oh, bollocks. Help pick these up for me?"

"Not my problem," Elbert yawns. "Last I checked this is my crypt. Not yours."

"And a lovely crypt it is."

"So, what. You want another game?"

"What else is there to do?"

"Fair enough. Load the artillery."

They played awhile. It seemed Twiner had upped his game considerably. It became quite a serious endeavour. People were even watching from behind the oblong slit. It was a whole thing. The disembodied rain continued to pour. Both factions were contorting in so many directions it almost seemed as if the unlimited possibilities had already been reached. Bishops fell, pawns were obliterated, bowmen on fortified castle roofs plucked queens into the dirt. Until, in one glorious move, whilst all he had was a solitary knight, Elbert ended the game, stampeding Twiner's king into the ground with a final flick of the wrist. Behind the door, an uproar of muffled applause. Everyone clapping.

"Good game, Lars."

"Best two out of three?"

"I'd love to, but I have a Meeting."

"Alright, old boy. I'll see you later."

"I hope not." Lars opened the door, and people were still huddled about outside. One of them was peering in especially strangely.

"Elbert?"

"..."

"Are you in there?"

"Who's that?"

"Lucy. It's Lucy," she mumbles as Twiner leaves. "Lucy Smith. I'm new. Just got here a few hours ago. I heard you were going to be around here, and I'm a big fan of you and your work."

"And what work would that be?"

"The Godhead." Elbert sat up.

"You know about that?"

"You're one of my heroes, actually. And then I happened to see that great game through the window. It was the work of a master. Could you give me a game? I would love it so much. Things are scary here. I don't really know anyone."

"Sorry, Lucy. I have an important meeting about now. And then I really need to take a snooze. Find me later on, I'll give you a game then."

"Okay. Thanks." The young woman left, beaming from ear

to ear. Elbert let out a chunky old sigh. He reached for his cane and drew himself up, and headed for reception. On the way, he noted the blur of Dev Dwyer in the Chill Out Room again. He waved to the kid and Dwyer replied with his own wave, though it still seemed like he thought any second the roof was going to blow. I mean, maybe he was right, though. Regardless, there wasn't time to find out. Making the Meeting on time was paramount. He had to prove he was adjusted. Even though in his own mind he adjusted a long time ago. He would be the first to admit he needed help in the beginning. And for good reason. But the fact of the matter was Elbert eventually did turn the tide and get better, after a few months. They just didn't think so. One of the things they liked to illuminate was the whole Orbo thing. Why, for instance, would a grown man, who is not in need of help, nor using any kind of MP, nor dreaming, nor even daydreaming, nor ignorant, nor high, nor religious, believe — truly — that there is a fairy in his dome? The general consensus being that such an individual must be mad. Or else a liar. But he wasn't. He wasn't mad, or lying. Since the doctor in question was a fresh recruit, he had to relay all the relevant information once more. And so he told her. How it all came to happen.

In the interim, in her newly appointed crypt, Luna Sterling covertly pulls a glass blue bag out of her midriff. She wipes the mobile and turns it on.

"Cain," she whispers. "I got him. Three weeks of simultaneously incarcerating myself in- and breaking out of- nearly every madhouse in Southern England . . . and I bloody well got him. White Water. Said I was hallucinating and afraid I was gonna hurt myself. Yeah. Had to cut up my arms a bit beforehand. Thing is, now I've got a taste for it. Yeah, I know. Well, he had a meeting to go to. Then a nap. Just what I was thinking. Would be. No. I know how to use it for Christ's sake. I'm not an idiot. Listen, you just tell M I'll have his precious code. Uh huh. At the latest. Alright, now to shove this phone back up my nether regions. Peace."

"Okay. Wow. That's very interesting."

"It's not meant to be interesting."

"Let me just get this straight. You made the device. And it drove you to insanity? Is that true? It wasn't any other reason?"

"What other reason would there be?"

"Well, there are various th —"

"Look. Please, just listen to me. I know it's why. Like I said,

I got it up and running, and everything was fine. I could see everything in great detail. But when I —"

"But when you?"

"But when I realised it was the only thing I *could* see . . . Well, just imagine for a second, doctor. Imagine that you are nearly completely blind. You lost your right eye years ago, and now the other eye is starting to turn, too. And all of a sudden there is a machine that allows you to see. Clearer than crystal. Yet the thing is, it doesn't allow you to see the real world. It allows you to see the machine. The homepage. The screen. Imagine that was all you could see. The screen. And nothing but. That's the rub, doctor. Either darkness, or a screen. And it got to me. I didn't want to see it that way. I wanted to see the world, and I thought this would do it. But it's not the world. It's a screen. And so I decided then, I decided I would rather see nothing than live this way. I turned it off, dropped the project. For good. Yet by then it had already done too much damage. I broke down, I suppose. Wasn't sleeping or making much sense to my wife. I just wanted to see again. It only blinded me further. And then Orbo came, in the darkness, and I knew it was real because the Godhead had long been uninstalled."

"Orbo being the phone's icon assistant."

"It's a living thing. It speaks to me, and I listen. It doesn't make me crazy. It doesn't make me mad. It came from the Godhead. And now it's in my head. Not that I understand why. I haven't turned that thing on in years. Yet still it's there."

"Inside your head?"

"Inside my head."

"Okay. I'm not here to ridicule your feelings, Elbert. But do you think that, since this being is talking to you, that there might be something else going on? Psychologically?"

"I do not claim to understand it. All I am saying is that it is true."

"Can I ask, when you found yourself in this state, did you admit yourself into the hospital?"

"I was teaching a lecture at the university. The Phenomenology of Chess. All this'd been going on for a while. I didn't tell anybody. I don't really remember the events, you know. I was informed by third parties."

"What happened?"

"Apparently I was grabbing the students, making them move around. Like chess pieces. Girl to D4. Boy to B7."

"I see."

"And I guess that just drove the point home that I was

losing my sense. But I've been well for quite a spell now. My daughter came last month and we conversed just fine. But I still haven't seen Little Ori, not for years. He's probably already Big Ori by now, and here I am, missing it all." Elbert sunk his head. There was a tear dripping from the eye patch.

XXVI

By February's end — aided by Luna Sterling's

sterling infiltration of DIPHU and her obtaining of the elusive executive master code via a black market neural analysis on a snoozed out Elbert Moon, the code being a twenty three digit number which when relayed to the MIND would allow one to gain total access of every other MIND — hundreds of towns all over the country had already implemented various domebending TRIPs of their own, until even the cities started getting involved, including but not limited to Leeds, Bristol, Manchester, Canterbury, and London. This was the lay of the land. Now anyhow. As more and more people were guided into the vast array of complexes, the real ace up the sleeve in furthering their plan was not simply being able to hack all active MPs with subliminal audio but being able to hack them with subliminal *cogito*. Also known as psyche sinkers . . . On the day the entire nation was finally under Illumine control, an eternally deep rolling arcus cloud seized the London skyline. Nobody looked up at it.

Mac Lorentz's sordid scheme of getting the whole of Britain's neck under his knee, which on the face of it made him seem not sordid at all but in fact gracious and daring, was once again backed by Pearly and the Kelpster, and not forgetting Leonard Swan either, the cherry faced poster boy of Mindphone Co. who struck a lucrative arrangement with Lorentz and the Spa for reasons of mutual compatibility. Swan came down to Illumine HQ and everything. There were herds of cameraheads in every conceivable direction that day. He'd opined to Cain and Sterling in private that if folk were ever to stay put at the Hotels — and due to the fact that it could not be achieved in any obviously authoritarian fashion or else no one would allow it in the first place — then supplying the guests of the Resort with their own psyche sinked MPs, again in gratis, could potentially cement their willingness to stay put, since an installed MIND had pretty much as many places to go as stars in the observable universe. All plethoric. All a mosaic. There was always something to escape into. It was its whole gimmick. And so you didn't actually have to be anywhere. You could be nowhere, in a crypt, in a sauna, in a cave, in a gutter, and lo and behold — the stars are out. Dead, and glimmering.

Out in the abandoned Mupfield Market, where people used to yell about plums and apricots just off the local franchise of the also abandoned Chicken Chonky, a great big Mindphone Co. holobanner lay eerily above the disused restaurant bearing a recursive image of Leonard Swan, of which underneath bore the neon lit words:

DON'T FORGET YOUR MONTHLY
CRANIAL CHARGE UP.
HAVE PEACE OF MIND, WITH MINDPHONE.

As the high streets became ever more idle, and in order to supply the Hotels with all the nourishment that would be needed, the carceral systems of England were bulldozed down and replaced with large scale agricultural farms. These Farms were then operated by the prisoners that had once been housed in the penitentiaries, and whose production sustained the Hotels' soaring demands for food. Every side flanked by armed guards, search lights and electric fences. In regards to the civilian population, it was decreed that mansions and second homes would be allowed to remain, while all other housing be swiftly replaced. The only exceptions to the rule, for reasons of convenience, were of the hospitals, the government offices and the mental institutions, all of which maintained their usual activity. Introduced also was the rather ignoble practice of allowing the wealthy alone access to the outside world. All they'd need to do was show their Illumine VIP pass to the front desk and they'd be allowed to leave. The hundredaires on the other hand were basically just stuck there. Skint and minted and such. But they never seemed to mind. And concerning the Dept. of Perambulation, headed by the filthiest Tory on the island, Gerrard Spank — hands became tied and they were forced to announce the department was closing for an indeterminate time. Perhaps perambulation was becoming an old antiquated philosophy, he'd said to the press. Hard to justify its continuance in an Illuminated world. It was only a few days however after the announcement that Old Spank'd had a bit of a levitating lightbulb thing going on in his melon when he clocked that just by changing one letter, one solitary letter of the department's name, they could not only remain in situ but avoid altogether the fact that — due to Illumine and Mindphone's recent symbiosis — no one either needed to move around any more nor wanted to move around any more, and that in medias res their department (and perhaps consequently their government) had effectively become obsolete. And so, with nothing more than a simple swap around, re the E and the R, Spank and his flock went from the Department of Perambulation to the ever more vague Department of Preambulation. Like the arcus cloud in London Town, nobody seemed to notice.

A road down the way from the holobanner of Swan, a group of ardent protesters — among them the fiery Rupy Mala, Ori's angel voiced friend — take to the streets holding cardboard placards scribed with FREE ORI MOON and ORI MOON IS INNOCENT and ABOLISH XENOPHOBIA and THE POLICE DIDN'T PROTECT HIM SO WHY WOULD THEY PROTECT US and ENGLAND CANT DENY ITS RACIST ROOTS ANY LONGER and FREE ORI MOON again and ORI MUST BE FREED and DOWN WITH SLAVE FARMING and STOP THE ARMS DEALS and WE LOVE YOU ORI and TO HELL WITH PEARLY and TO

HELL WITH THE TORIES and WE STAND WITH ORI and IT WAS ONE TUBE OF GLUE and TO HELL WITH THE TORIES again and ORI MUST BE FREED again and WE LOVE ORI and FREE ORI . . .

When feds eventually bowled up to the scene, the protesters were beaten with metal truncheons and taken to the Farms. They were never seen again. Up on Hatchers Lane, Burgess Moon, who'd witnessed the event through his flat window, was now in bed looking down at a letter, gripping it ironclad tight. In what can only be described as a scrawl, the letter read:

To Burgess, my son.

Burgess, I wish you would come to Dosborough House and see your old man. I miss you deeply. Please don't be afraid of coming down. Everyone here is good as gold. Don't be afraid. I love you more than anything. You are my boy, and I will always be proud of you. I know it seems we've grown apart, and I guess we have, but you are always in my mind and heart. I hope you get this letter. I don't really know if they post these things. But I would like to think they do. Sending all my love.
P.S. Please excuse my handwriting, I am having trouble making

it legible.

Elbert

After he finished reading it, he read it again. And then again. It was more trying to decipher the scrawl than anything. When he got to the ellipsis on the third attempt, a thick chunky noise emanating from the street outside entered his eardrums. He moved his curtains aside and peered out the bedroom window. It was a JCB. With eerie portent, the intercom buzzed. Turned out today was the day. Burgess went outside and talked to the demolitionist. The guy said he and everyone else who lived in the flat better be out by noon otherwise they were going to wake up with a roof for a duvet. Burgess nodded. He offered the guy a coffee related proposition but the guy declined. Strange. You'd think demolitionists would love a good old cup of coffee.

"So," the guy says. "Anything you want to keep we have to take out now. Put it in the back of a van, store it for you if you want. That'll cost extra, though."

"Extra? You mean, this is costing me?"

"Hey, I don't make the rules."

"No, right."

"Are you excited to move into your new place, then?"

"You mean the complex? Oh, sure."

"You'll love it. I moved in just last week. They got the nicest pools you've ever seen. Like swimming in a sea of diamonds."

"Sounds relaxing."

"..."

"So they still let you work for the council, then?"

"I'm a key worker. It's essential work, this what I'm doing."

"No doubt, no doubt. Hey, you know that MP shop up on the high street? Is that place considered essential?"

"MP Mania? Don't see why it would be. It's all delivery now."

"Right."

"You liked the place, eh?"

"No, I hated it."

"Listen, lad. You can be honest with me. You bloody loved that job. Can tell just from your face how gutted you are about it. You bloody loved that job, am I right or am I right?"

"I —"

"Bloody loved it." After that, the guy just randomly

wandered off. The JCB was still there, left idle on the street. Burgess shook his head and went back inside.

It later turned out that the demolitionist just had to pop and get some fags from the offy, coming back around noon all locked and loaded. As he walked up to the flat he unsheathed a snout, stationing it betwixt his gob, then looked over his shoulder and suddenly went all quiver lipped, the fag falling out his mouth. The JCB was gone. Again the intercom buzzed.

"Ahoy hoy."

"*Where* is it?"

"Where's what?"

"My fucking JCB!"

"Your JCB? What do you mean? Is it not there?"

"Don't play dumb with me you little shit, I know it was you!"

"Sorry, but how can I have stolen your JCB? I'm in my flat."

"I guess that makes sense . . . Look, can you just come down for a minute. Maybe you saw something. Also there's someone from Illumine down here that wants to talk."

"Alright." He turned away from the intercom, grabbing an

item from his desk, and ventured for the exit.

"Huh," Burgess says, now outside. "It really is gone."

"Did you see anything then?"

"Sorry. Didn't see anything." At that moment, the aforementioned Illumine representative shouldered up to Burgess.

"Mr. Moon? Jason Lorvo. I've come to escort you to your new living space."

"Oh, how nice." The demolitionist lost all his remaining patience and wandered off yet again, haranguing people on the street as to the whereabouts of his JCB.

"Let's walk," Lorvo says. They walked. "So. You've been working at an MP shop, correct?"

"That's me."

"I guess it's a shame you have to hand in the towel."

"It's a damn shame, Jason. A damn shame."

"Well. Onwards and upwards." He put a hand on Burgess's shoulder. "It's not like MPs will be out of your life forever. We are very strongly supportive of the notion that our workers should always have access to their MP, even on shifts."

"Great."

"What model are you using, out of curiosity?"

"85Z."

"85Z? I haven't heard of an 85Z."

"X. Meant to say X."

"And it's all installed and working?"

"That it is, J man. That it is." Lorvo looked down at the item in his hand.

"Is that all you're taking with you?" he says. "An old Game Boy?"

"All I'm taking."

"Where'd you manage to get one of those?"

"Found it on the bus."

"Those are pretty rare these days."

"What can I say, J dog. Everything's finally coming up roses."

After Lorvo had escorted him into his Hotel room, Burgess mused on whether this was the best tactic he could have taken. Walking deep into the eye of the hurricane. Yet by all accounts if she was going to be anywhere it was probably going to be here. He hid the Game Boy Color under his pillow and left the room for the Hotel bar. Several floors below his unbeknownst feet, down in an arid and gloomy oubliette, an unapprehended Delphine Moon, chained by the neck with a steel collar, is studying her own schnoz intently. Hilton Dax is on the other side of her, also chained by the neck, looking dead to the world. She gazed over at him via the faint neon light jutting down from the slits in the high trap door.

"Hilton. You awake, Hilton?"

"..."

"Oi." She jutted out her booted heel and nudged him in the thigh. "You can't possibly be sleeping now."

"..."

"What a peculiar human being."

"Eh..." he says, finally lifting his lids.

"Why are you taking a fucking nap?"

"Shattered. Plus, your perfume made me dozy."

"I'm not wearing perfume, you melon."

"Damn. That's all you?"

"Look, Dax. We've gotta get our heads out of our arses here."

"What do you suggest?"

"I don't know. Stay conscious?"

"Consciousness is overrated," he says, yawning. "It's the reason we're here for Christ's sake. We couldn't be washed by the psyche sinkers."

"Precisely. We couldn't be washed. We've still got our faculties. Enough to make it out of here. Even your dopey arse."

"Is this really about making it out of here? Or do you just want another hit of nicotine."

"Two birds, Dozy. Two birds."

XXVII

Deep in the heart of the badlands, more

commonly referred to as the Communal Lounge of Dosborough Independent Psychiatric House Unit's Butterfly Ward — a place that after nearly six weeks Kira Mizuki is strangely starting to call Home — a conversation brews around the big coffee table between a couple of Newly Planted Flowers. One of them's this robed bipolar gentleman called Charlie Volair who has a perfectly elliptical head, a neophyte of not only the House but also of the Twisted Buddhas' Sleep Awakening Cult of Kinship; the other Flower an anhedonic schizophrenic named Amelia Cadhan who can't help but mistake the guy for a shadow that's somehow disentangled itself from the confines of the wall. Volair isn't particularly upset with what she's saying, he simply refuses to admit he is a two dimensional absence of light. He was in here for excessive twisted buddhahood and that was that. Cut him some slack, chimes Duke, sitting on his chair in a wilted lotus position. He was listening to a Sony Walkman which he found in the lost and found eight years ago. Inaudible to old Duke, Mizuki sneezed a big old sneeze. No one said gesundheit. Only Duke said stuff like gesundheit to people, and he was busy listening to his Walkman. Mizuki reckons sneezes are not devils flying out your snout so much as fairies. When they come out through the old *kushami* they never come back, and when you're old and you die is when all of the fairies have left. It's a long story how she came to the conclusion. Maybe one day Mizuki will tell you.

So old Charlie Voliar of the Twisted Sack arrangement was saying no, no, he was not a shadow, but a man, standing upright in a black and yellow robe reminiscent of bees (and Mizuki loves bees, they are fat and ever so tiny at the same time. Like stars in the sky. Or black holes. Mizuki is happy when she think of the bumblebees for instance, and there's nothing wrong with that. Mizuki is strange but now so is everyone else, everyone's a butterfly in Butterfly Ward. Everybody's everybody. Mizuki Mizuki. Duke Duke. Noirel Noirel. Medium Nigel Medium Nigel. And on . . .). Old

Cadhan was having none of it, this talk of the shadow being not a shadow but a man, until Volair touched her gently on the shoulder and she clocked his higher dimension.

Even though it was a communal lounge people tended to get up and walk about a lot of the times. Stillness was rare. The only other options you even really had were going back to your crypt, or else subdued and entwined on the metal fence in a botched breakout. And so folk fluctuated, like subatomic particles. The frozen folk were considered either bodhisattvas or goners was the general agreement. It was a dangerous game to play. Staying still in a place like this. Basically like grenading your own mouth, someone who went by Lucy Smith said to her one afternoon while Mizuki was walking by reception. Haven't seen her since. Might've been transitioned to Pepsi, or Saturn. Maybe another madhouse entirely.

Mizuki sneezed again. She thought about the words house & mad and when you put them together you get madhouse. Mad is a nice word both originally or reversed so madhouse is not derogatory term to Mizuki. Mad is good. It's one letter away from being made. She told that to Duke, who replied jovially that madness cannot be created or destroyed. He'd wilted completely by this juncture, his tree trunk legs outstretched on the carpeted floor with a *Mupfield Advertiser* held right above his dark craned dome, concerning himself with the news of the day. He flipped the pages back and forth and jutted out a digit.

FLAT MATE WANTED

LOOKING FOR CONGENIAL HOUSE MATE FOR TWO BED FLAT IN DOSBOROUGH AVENUE

RENT £399 PCM

ASSASSINS WELCOME

NO SMOKERS (OR PETS)

"There's some messed up stuff in the news," he says, templeshaking. Simone Noirel then came into view, transmogrifying herself into the chair adjacent to Mizuki. When was it ever *not* messed up, she chimed. The girl was clad in a black cardy and had a rollup on her ear, hair darker than intergalactic space. Mizuki knocked tentatively on the old cranium, and Noirel amicably returned the gesture. She looked a bit more content today, from what could be deduced by Mizuki. She was going on about a scientifically created vegan beef burger she ate in the mess hall at lunch, and that she ate the whole thing. Everyone cheered for her. Go Simone this and Go Simone that. Someone else, though, a paranoiac friend of Medium Nigel's, thought the folk were saying Go as in Go Away, and had to be told it was the opposites.

After the NPFs had settled down, they were escorted by ward security to Pill Manor for their introductory doses. Mizuki got some pharmacologicals down her own gullet after a short conk in her crypt about an hour later. She'd been dreaming of the sparkly skirt. She'd been dreaming of Kyoto. Being in Kyoto in her sparkly skirt.

Elsewhile, as soundwaves of rain poured over the land, outside it had actually begun raining for true. Simone, unaware of the rain outdoors but deeply aware of the rain indoors, yielded that she'd been having nightmares about being drowned. Medium Nigel interjected he'd been having nightmares, too. And that after the nightmare he would go to sleep. Duke read more of the paper, again in his old aleatory fashion. The resulting page:

ILLUMINE SPA SET TO BECOME WORLDWIDE WITH
GLOBAL RESORT INTEGRATION PROGRAMME.
SOMETHING SOMETHING SOMETHING.

While he was indeed curious about what was going on outside the confines of the ward, Duke found it hard to read much more than the headline. He chucked the newspaper aside in such a manner that it did not fragment into pieces — musing on how if you lived with an assassin they'd probably be really quiet around the flat and not get in your way or anything — and went out to the Playground for a smoke of fresh air. The rain was falling. Falling on the Flowers.

XXVIII

Contused Neil had an unfathomable headache.

He breathed in through the bag. They had taken his skateboard when he arrived. Said there was a great MP game he could play instead. Only five hundred credits. That way he could skate wherever he wanted. In his Hotel room.

On the big mounted television, a video of Mac Lorentz blares against the silence. He's on a flying carpet. As you would be.

"We at Illumine believe you deserve to relax," he says. "That's why we've created the most relaxing place in the entire world. Five star facilities, impeccable staff — the Illumine Spa Resort is a place for all, and with easy to access cranial charge ups, soundproof rooms, exotic cuisine and drink, glistening pools and saunas — every desire is a quenchable one." (Mac takes a sip of his cocktail.) "Now . . .

that's goooood drambuie." With an impish wink at the camera, the video loops back to the beginning. "We at Illumine believe you deserve to relax . . ."

He huffed on the bag some more. Unknown to him, Lorentz was not actually there on the holographic TV but on his own private island far away in the Indian Ocean, lying down in a floating recliner with his associate Luna Sterling, cashing in on his winnings, which were indeed immense. At one point or another, there was a rap on the door. He hid the bag down his trousers and told them it was open.

"Mosh?" It was Pillsly. "What you saying, man?"

"Bag," he says, pulling it out and taking another gargantuan huff.

"I see you're enjoying yourself."

"..."

"Do you think it's a good idea to be doing so much of that?"

"Sit down and have a bag with me."

"I've quit."

"You quit? Now why would you go and do that? Medzo's gonna come down."

"Yulian's dead, if you forgot."

"I didn't fucking forget. I'm doing this precisely because I didn't forget."

"What the hell happened to you? Where's my friend Neil gone? Where is he? You used to *care* about shit. You dug the *Event* Horizon. And you never complained. That's what you used to be like." Mosh reapplied the bag, and took a rather quite nasty blob straight up through his nasal canal.

"I don't want to lose you, too."

"Already lost."

"Okay. Have fun with your bag." Pillsly left. Neil turned off the TV and cried.

As Flynn walked down the corridor, they passed a woman with a great red mane and a coiled port palm round the neck of a gilded bottle. It was the mane of Florence Pipelli, coming back from the shower room, still in her towel. She removed the I.D. key from her teeth and vanished through the door. Pillsly kept walking.

After she was all cleaned and clad, Florence was back to work, using her new 85X to load up the manuscript. The title was all she had so far. The Bubbles. She kept adding a word and then deleting a word. She'd never before felt both so relaxed and yet so tense. What words could she write that would change anything? What words could save, save the words of Christ or Buddha? Yet then again, maybe they didn't have to save. Maybe they just needed to be said. Jotted with a bubble wand.

Meanwhile, down in the cleaning cupboard, a psyche sinked Francesca Ianni hangs up robes with a perpetual RBF. By the back door of the cupboard, the also psyche sinked Buck Da Luz is utilising a heavy engine machine to power wash the floor of all the cigarettes and grime. Flint's snorting smoke clouds she's so creased up.

"Wanna take over, Soph?" he says. "I'm getting pretty knackered using this thing."

"Love to mate, but my medication says I'm not allowed to use heavy machinery."

"Jammy bastard. I need to start taking what you're taking. Where the hell's Del and Dax?" At that juncture the machine cut out. Buck dropped it on the ground and joined Flint and her fading purple highlights in their heavenbent endeavour of killing time, unsheathing snouts for one more final smoko, returning to the fire of apocatastasis, returning to the flames, weird and wingless angels.

XXIX

Once upon a time, once upon a boat. A fishing
boat to be specific. In summertime. Not a drop of rain. Him
and his dad. Old Jupp. He was teaching him how to catch
fish with just a piece of bait and a fishing line. They'd gone
to find little shellfish on nearby rocks for the bait, and he
watched his father jump across the bow and gather and haul
back a big bag of bait, proceeding to deshell them with a
toffee hammer and chuck the remains in a bucket. It was fun
to watch him balance himself on the sole of the boat,
bringing in the anchor or tying ropes in mystical myriads,
the sun above his head like a celestial hat. He bent down and
moved one of the wooden paddles aside to clear some space
on the deck.

"Will you look at that, Elbert," he says. "That's going to be a great area to put all my catches. What do you think? Are you going to beat me today?"

"..."

"I don't think you'll be able to beat me, you know."

"Uh huh."

"Elbert. Are you even listening? Don't you want to fish?"

"But I've nearly solved my Rubik's Cube." He displayed it to his father. Jupp grabbed it and pretended to throw it overboard. It was funny because he didn't actually throw it. Jupp was nice like that most of the time. He said you can play with that thing for twenty more seconds and then we're going to start our little competition here what do you say my son and so after twenty or so seconds Elbert finally decided to chuck his line out and fish with him, even though he thought it was stupid to fish. But when Jupp started pulling up all these catches — like thirteen by a quarter hour — Elbert finally thought maybe it wasn't so stupid. They would have food to eat that night because of how good the old man was. Maybe enough for their friends, too. He talked about the line as like a string on a musical instrument, that you had to feel the vibration and react at the right time, that it was like a dance, a nautical dance, a special note on a waterproof piano. He thought his dad was just bragging about how good he was at catching fish with his fishing line, but truth of the matter Jupp just found it fascinating to think about, having been a fisherman all his life and ever since his own father, Eli, took him boating in the old Düsum waters in 1949. The sea they shared. The gunmetal sea.

After an hour, as dawn metamorphosed to morning, Jupp had caught around fifty five fishes. Elbert was trailing behind at a lowly zero. In Roman times, he'd at least have caught one. But it wasn't Roman times. Distracted, he played with the Cube in his pocket. He was aligning all the colours in the darkness, and as he pulled it out a moment later with his starboard hand — the port hand still held tight to the nylon line — he saw that all the colours were aligned correctly. He could do that, but he couldn't catch a fish. If it really were Roman times, he'd be dead in a week. I mean, what use is a Rubik's Cube in the Colosseum.

As the morning melted into noon, just as the dawn had melted into morning, a swirl of rain clouds began to apparate over the zenith of the boat, rippling the watertop. It was really chucking down. Elbert thought perhaps it was a sign from God that it didn't want Old Jupp to empty the sea any further. Still, he held on tight to the nylon, watching his father pull out catch after catch until it nearly capsized the damn boat. It wasn't like Elbert particularly wanted to catch anything. He just wanted to be like Jupp. And so he held on tight, waiting, waiting, waiting, and when the line finally happened to tug back, and the rain on high was falling fiercer than ever, he pulled up the nylon with his little hands, until a squid came up and inked him right in the face, and his eyes were lacquered with ink, and he told his father he was blind and couldn't see, and Old Jupp just started laughing, bringing down an empty bucket to the water's edge and bringing it up again and splashing Elbert's eyes with it, and then Elbert was laughing, because he realised he wasn't blinded, and that he still had both his eyes, and at that moment, he arose in his crypt in Pepsi Ward, in the middle of night, and Orbo was there waving its wings, and the rain was still falling. Chucking down from the speakers.

XXX

It was a cool March evening on the Farm. Ori Moon,

who'd been assigned to a horticultural endeavour, was just finishing up sowing a bunch of spinach seeds into the hydrochronic containers. The air was cold yet fresh, a whole lot nicer than the prison air. But it was still a prison of sorts. Up in the overworld where the glare of a nearby SkyScreen fell harsh into his orbs, a gibbon moon looked down on him and his cohorts, hanging from an invisible tree. He was tired. Not no seed anymore. Just a big bulging fruit. And if you wait around long enough the fruit goes bad and rots away and dies, and then the fruit goes to heaven or the fruit goes to hell, which is the same place anyway. Ori hopes in any case that when he does rot away, he rots away with some sort of contentment. Feeling grateful to have lived at all. Because the only thing worse than dying is dying in a bad mood.

He packed away his kit and wandered back to his quarters with an armed guard following his every step. They had to be armed just in case any workers managed to get over the electrified fences. It was a sad place. Dolarous. Somehow though, and luckily, he'd made a compadre to help him see some semblance of beauty in the sadness. Her name was Joy Something. She was a journalist who worked for a news show. He asked her how she came to be at the Farm. She said to Ori that she was here because she told the truth, and some people didn't like the fact she did that, tell the truth and such, and these people were powerful and had lots of money and they didn't like the truth so much. Then she asked Ori how he came to be at the Farm, and he told her it wasn't as interesting as her story but what happened was they took Ori over an alleged theft of a tube of Constitutionally Loco he'd got from the Hub. Though it didn't make much sense to Ori, it seemed to make some sense to her. She asked why Constitutionally Loco and he said it was to fix his time machine. It wasn't a joke but she chuckled anyhow, thinking he was being witty or something. Ori understands it's hard for folk to wrap their head around. He doesn't blame them. If they end up

213

laughing, well, that just means there's something nice to listen to. Like birdsong. Caged in C.

When Joy Something left to conk out for the night, with the armed guard right on his tale, Ori walked as slothy as he could get away with. It wasn't nice having to go back in. As he entered his cell he got to thinking about the Moons. Not the lunar object orbiting Dirt, or the moons of Jupiter or Satern — but the folk who had taken him in. He missed them a lot. All that time together. And not just the time together but the time itself . . . And yet it's always been there. Not linearly but lunarly. Life isn't linear, Ori doesn't think. He reckons it's more a crazy spiral. Wrapped around the head.

XXXI

Cosmetic?"

"Kismetic."

"It hardly seems kismetic, Delph."

"That's what I thought, too. Then it hit me. Maybe it got to all this *because* I wasn't stopping with the cigarettes. Maybe God put me here to *save* my arse. I mean, sure, I might have been free out there. But it was snout central, Dax. It took a ruddy kidnapping to stop me from tarring up my lungs. If that's not kismetic I don't know what the hell is." Hilton looked off to the side, seemingly unswayed by her reasoning. It wasn't completely unfounded. Thanks to his method of hashmarking every accountable second on the starboard wall with a pointed pebble that'd come off the stony ground, he knew they had only been there a few hours. Just wait until the night passes, he felt like saying. Obviously he didn't. He was too intimidated by her. She had a stare like molten lava when she was ticked off. All volcanic and such. Probably best to leave the volcano alone. He was afraid of what she might do. Even if it was just a roll of the eyes. Those eyes of molten lava. With that molten lava look. If only they could use it to melt the chains. The ironic thing was that he'd been studying metallurgy for the past four years. Needless to say, the knowledge was quite useless without any tools.

After reciting her benzo mantra — getting to three hundred and twenty seven this time before realising she was actually ODing on the mantra, and that three hundred and twenty seven mantras was too many mantras — Delphine cracked her fingers, thinking about her cat Shlomo. Just lying there. Just being Shlomo. It made her want to cry. Hilton meanwhile had drifted off to sleep again, curled inward with his temple on the ground. The guy could conk out wherever. Name the place, he could conk out there. Couldn't blame him to be honest. Couldn't blame anyone. Not even herself. Not even Lorentz. A little bit Lorentz.

The withdrawal from the nicotine was getting horrid

again. Everytime she craved a snout she thought about Shlomo to stave it off, even though smoking was a physical impossibility anyway. Hilton woke up at some juncture or another, started saying he had a dream about the Big Rip.

"So, not a nightmare about the Big Rip?"

"Oh no, it was a nightmare. There were these cats . . . being ripped apart by space. First the fucking planet tore apart, then the country tore apart, then the city tore apart, and then the pubs, then the people, then the dogs, then the cats, then the bees, then the particles, and then, when all that had torn apart, spacetime tore apart. Fucking *spacetime*, Del. Cats and the goddamn Minkowski space."

"Speaking of felines and spacetime — hey, that would make a good band name — I miss Shlomo."

"Eh, Shlomo shmomo." To the untrained ear it sounded like Dax wasn't taking into account Delphine's feelings for Shlomo with that line — but he was smiling when he said it and just seemed to want to use the shm-reduplication for its own sake. Delphine got bolted in the forehead by another craving. She kept unwantedly thinking about the Iris Incident. Those patches would have come in real handy right about now.

"Hilton," she says. "I need some help over here."

"Shoot."

"What's your interpretation of string theory?"

"That's what you need help with?"

"Did I ask you if you were a bitch, or did I ask you for your interpretation of string theory?"

"You're mean when you're hot." Immediately Dax pictured molten lava in his cranium.

"You're weird when you're weird. Seriously, what do you think about it, though?"

"I think that the universe is a piano. And we are the notes." He reached out and held her meat hook in the darkly oubliette. "We are the notes."

XXXII

At the gloaming hour, Burgess Moon — lone

Luddite, phonebox dweller extraordinaire, poster boy for the paranoid — lies supine on his silky Hotel bed with his yellow Game Boy Color held superjacent to his dome. His resolve had diminished considerably since being unable to find D anywhere. But goddamn was it comfortable in that bed. That was the whole problem. You never wanted to get out.

He'd played on the Game Boy for so long it needed new batteries. He put it down, and picked up the hyperglue. He'd got the glue from this girl called Jhoanne he'd met at the pool. She smelt like glue, as if that was her perfume. It was an in-&-out operation I guess you could say. Her bobbed cigarette holder kept brushing his forehead.

Unscrewing the lid, wearing a pair of medical gloves he'd nabbed from one of the first aid kits in the downstairs closet, Burgess carefully positioned the newly acquired tube of Constitutionally Loco not at a rag, or polythene bag, or even his honker or gob — but at the Hotel room door. It brought back permafrosted memories of hypergluing the KX100 back at the start of the year. God, had it really been two months? Illumine's Empire, raised in two solitary months? It took longer to get bloody hyperglue approved.

He put the tube down and looked out the window. Guards were circling the area below the glass jetty. If he could get past them, the forest was just up ahead. Beyond the forest a road, that if taken, would lead straight to Dosborough House.

After he'd put the new batteries in the Game Boy, he turned it on and left it on the table. He then proceeded to take all his clothes off, gathered every fibre up and knotted it all into one big rope. He tied it to the window latch and looked out again. The guards were still there. There was a rap on the door. He didn't hang around — he climbed out the window and abseiled down, fortuitously placed parallel to an evergreen. The knot he'd made was, however, unfortunately not strong enough to hold him, coming loose as he and the rope nosedived thirteen feet into a holly bush. The guards turned their melons to the noise.

"What was that?"

"I don't know." They walked over to the bush. One of the guards' MPs started ringing, and they paused to converse a while. Something to do with one of the guests locking themselves in their Hotel room. Post-inspection of the old bush, they concluded nothing here was awry, and schlepped off. It was only after they fell out of sight that Burgess ran, naked and scratched, to the forest edge. As he ebbed away amidst the viridian, they finally broke down the door, and, the guard, seeing the Game Boy Color on the table lighting up and producing song, became eminently distracted, and — as expected — started playing the game. Sitting on the bed and everything. In pure nostalgic hypnosis. By this time, of course, Burgess was deep into the forest's belly. There was just one small problem — he didn't know where the fuck he was going.

"Josh, put the Game Boy down, man."

"But if I use this Ice Beam TM now I might be able to catch the Drago-"

"JOSH."

"Okay, okay!"

Leaping desperately about the woodland freezed and half bewildered, Burgess settled down on a tiny tree stump. The moon was a mandala. Stars, too. He was quite distressed. He wiped his blurry optics. As he struggled to decipher the way, he heard in the distance what sounded like someone knocking on a door. But there was no door for this forest. He closed his lids and remained still. There it was again. A woodpecker? Not cognizant of which way to venture, he began following the aural trail, unfurling himself about the forest's arabesques. It seemed upon closer examination that the sound of the rapping was emanating from a particular tree just off to his left. When he got to the tree in question, there was a little tarsier perched on its bough munching on a beetle. One of the last lot of the zoological exodus, in fact. The little guy'd managed to make it this long. Burgess went over to say hi and but when the tarsier heard him coming it seized up and scurried to another bough of the tree. Then it started hitting its head on the tree trunk. Really going for it. Burgess didn't know why or what for, but it was because he'd startled it. It just kept headbutting the damn wood. In a way, he could relate. I mean, if he was a tarsier, and a human came up to him, he'd probably wanna headbutt a tree trunk, too. He backed away, in hope it would stop doing it. After a spell it seemed to relent. A few deep breaths came from its mouth, and finally it looked at him, right at him, with its spheric amberly eyes mandalic like the moon, and gone not two seconds later as it swivelled its dome and darted up the top of the tree. Hopefully, not to jump off. Skullfirst.

He resumed his trek, and after a lot of vacillation and oscillation, found an outward path up ahead, to which when schlepped, revealed he'd made it out the other side. As he neared ever closer in his mind the white waves of DIPHU, coming out of the foresty web and into the streetlit terra firma of Mupfield Town, Burgess suddenly clocked he was running about with no clothes on, tripping over something on the pavement in his discombobulation. He looked down. It was a hat. The hat of the girl in the Gengar hat.

Eventually, after his keen session of living off the lay of the land i.e. getting lost in a forest for the better part of three hours — Burgess was presently at the front door of Dosborough House, and bear in mind now that he was completely naked bar shoes and considerably scratched up from the holly bush, which, although seemed fortuitous for his aim of getting admitted, was merely a fateful accident. He progressed to bowl right on up and knock on the locked door. A few moments went by. He kicked his shoes a bit and looked down at the ground. Then came a voice. It was coming from the intercom on his right. He spoke into it and told them he was in need of help, that his name was Humboldt Bush and old Humboldt didn't know where his clothes went so he started scratching his body with a compass to notify the Underlords of his intentions to fulfil the Galactic Prophecy. And nothing more was said, they let him in, chucking a big blanket over him also whilst they looked for more appropriate clothes in the lost and found. What they came back with a short spell after was quite remarkable. An off white XXXL I.R. Baboon T-shirt with the words 'I.R. Baboon' written upside down on the shirt, and maybe even worst of all — a tight pair of bright green polyethylene jogging shorts. All they had apparently. It was either wear that or wear a gown. But that seemed even worse. He put the monkey on his back.

"So, Humboldt me lad," says the attending nurse, a lithe Irish woman with emerald eyes. "We're going to take you to Saturn Ward now that you're all up to date and got something to wear. That alright?"

"Saturn? It's just. Saturn scares me."

"It does, aye?"

"Yeah. And space scares me. I don't like looking up at it. Even thinking about it. It brings back all these terrible meteorites. I mean, memories."

"If you really feel so strongly me lad we could perhaps take you to Pepsi instead? I think they have some rooms available. Does Pepsi scare you?"

"No, I drink it every day. Love the stuff."

"Great. We'll take you to Pepsi then. Bear in mind there aren't actually any Pepsis to take."

"There aren't? Oh, that's okay. I need to cut down anyway."

When Burgess had been fully admitted and roomed under the nebulously derived nom de plume Humboldt Bush, he went looking for his old man. He'd been to visit him so little he couldn't even remember the room number. It didn't make him feel good. The letter apparated through his dome. Well, he was here wasn't he? Strange circumstances notwithstanding, he was here.

He ventured outside the small cream cube of the room. Was he supposed to leave? It's not like they locked the door or anything. He took a right as he left the threshold and followed the long corridor down, seeing all the makeshift

A4 paper signs of the patients' names on their respective crypt doors. There were a few of them that didn't even have a name. One simply said DO NOT ENTER. Another said I'M WITH STUPID with an arrow pointing starboard. And the other said HEAVEN (mine).

As he turned yet another corner, Burgess passed a wider door with the words CHILL OUT ROOM scribed on a side panel. There was somebody in there in the fetal position shaking like a leaf and surrounded on all sides by several walls of books. It didn't seem like a good time to go in and introduce himself. He inclined his body back to the artery of the corridor, and when he swivelled round he made contact with somebody also swivelling round. In a green quilted jacket. And charcoal black patch.

"Sorry there, my friend."

"Dad?"

"Is that . . . No. I don't believe it. You're here!" He bent down and hugged him. "You finally came to visit me."

"Er, yeah. I came to visit you."

"Did the Hotel give you a lift up here then?"

"Can we talk somewhere more privately, Dad?"

"Let's go to my crypt," he says. "My boy! Finally coming to visit his old man!" He seemed really happy. It filled Burgess with shame.

"So, what have you been up to, my boy?" he asks as they schlep on down the ward's arterial.

"You know. Got a job . . . Slept in a phonebox . . . The usual."

"My boy," he says again, shaking his head and cracking a faint smile. "I guess I can be proud of one of those things. What do you say we play a game of chess when we go in?"

"I would like that. It's just, like I was saying before. I really need to speak to you about something." They reached his crypt. Elbert opened the door with his caneless hand and gestured him inside. The door slowly fanned across, shutting into the frame without a single noise, the only sounds audible seeming to be some really loud rainstorm outside. You could hear it all the way through the ward.

"So," he says. "What do you want to talk about, then?"

"It's about where Delphine works. The spa resort."

"Illumine?"

"I couldn't find her, Dad. When they took me there I tried to find her. I couldn't. No one knew where she was."

"That's curious."

"And I tied up all my clothes and made a rope, and threw it out the window and made a run for it. To find you. I didn't know who else to look for."

"So they didn't let you out?"

"They don't let anybody out. Not unless they've got enough money."

"How are they doing this, though? How are they getting away with it?"

"I think it has something to do with the Mindphones. I'm not sure." Elbert ruffled his forehead.

"I think I know what's going on," he says. "There's no choice. We have to intervene."

"Dad, I know you were the one who made the bloody thing. But this is bigger than us. There's no way to stop Illumine."

"Listen. Did I ever tell you about the story of me and my mother playing chess together?"

"Dad, I'm tryi —"

"My mother, your grandmother, told me this move in chess. The One Move Killer. Where you can end the game in one move. Do you know what that move is?"

"I don't know it, Dad . . ."

"You take the king, *your* king, and you knock it over. You sacrifice your king. Game over. One move. That's it."

"Surely that can't be a regulation move."

"No, you are right. It's not. But when it comes to life, the OMK is indeed a possible move."

"I don't know what you're getting at. I'm scared, Dad. I don't want to talk about chess right now."

"My son. There are things I haven't told you. I'm sorry for that. I guess now I ought to. When I created the Godhead, I made a contingency plan. Because I knew this device could possibly become very powerful, maybe even too powerful for the world to bear. When the prototype was stolen it seemed to be out of my hands. But it wasn't. Because I made a contingency plan. I had a secret code, a master code, allowing me alone control of the grid. It seems that that code has now been figured out. But that wasn't all I did. I developed a switch. A very tiny override switch, that if engaged, would shut down every Godhead in a single bound, bypassing the master code access. Full grid blackout. Illumine, I fear, are now using master coded MPs to hack into people's interfaces. To make them feel that they do indeed want to live in this kind of world. Subliminal cogito. And so there it is. There is an override switch. And all we have to do is turn it."

"You mean. You can really do that?"

"I can really do that. But I need your help, Burgess. I need you to do something very important for your old man. And it's not going to be pretty."

"What?"

"See that black book over there on the sill?"

"This one?"

"That's the one. Go ahead and open it." Burgess moved his hand to the book. It trembled.

"Now," he says. "See that thing in there. Take it out." He took it out. It looked like a piece of plumbing. "When I made the switch, I had to put it somewhere no one would think to look," he says. "Usually I would've been able to contact a surgeon and have anaesthetics at hand and all this, if I ever needed it removed. Obviously we don't have either of those. And yet, there is a chance, Burgess, a chance for you and me to make. Stop Illumine, shut down the grid . . . or let it grow, until not only are me and you and Dev in a crypt — everyone's in a crypt."

"I don't like where this is going."

"I would do it myself," he says. "But I can't lift my arms in the position that is needed." Burgess looked down at the trepan in his still trembling hook. Elbert raised his own hook and ran it down the back of his neck. "The occipital bone."

"The switch is . . . in situ?"

"In situ."

"And this is the only way?"

"Don't sound so sad, my boy."

"But you're asking me to kill you."

"No, I'm not asking that. There is a chance I will survive. If you can do it right."

"No. No!"

"Burgess. Please don't cry."

"Fuck you! You never spoke to me all my life! You played chess with me once! Once! Now you want me to . . . You *are* crazy. Fucking crazy!"

"I'm sorry. I should have spoken to you more. I'm sorry, my boy."

"This has to be a nightmare . . . I shouldn't have come." Elbert was still sitting up on the bed. Burgess almost left the room but hesitated. Looking at his father's face, the wrinkly skin scarred by acid, his big Germanic brown dog eye, the missing eye veiled in felt, his hair as white as ice — it froze him in his place. After a spell, he looked back down at the hollowed out book on his lap and the trepan he was still now wielding. The sacrifice of the king . . . Queerly, there seemed a moment where the trembled hand stopped trembling. He went over to the bed and said if it had to be done then it had to be done. He followed his father's every instruction, guiding him to the occipital bone where the switch so tempestuously lay behind. After it had all sunk in as much as it could, the surgery began. Burgess made Elbert hold his hand.

"Keep going, my boy. Keep going." And he abided. And abided. And abided. The mystic rain trickling down. He kept on drilling, aiming for as straight an angle as possible. And he abided. And he abided. And he abided.

By the hour, the drill was beginning to gather a vast amount of blood as it finally and ominously pierced through the far side of the cranium. Elbert didn't say anything after that.

When the trepanning was over, Burgess was still holding his hand. He put the saw back in the hollow book and gazed into the incision, pulling out thereafter a thin plasticky looking sheet bearing a small protrusion. He looked down at it, squinting. There were two tiny words scribed on the sheet. ON on the right. OFF on the left. He flipped the panel portside, and all at thunderous once, that tenacious hellbent worldwide whir — that whir that expanded and whorled the skull, trapping it in luxury, entombing it in gold — now broke free from the chains of sound and dropped to a silence unhallowed. He was still holding onto the hand. There was no movement, even the very Earth seemed to rest in place. When he finally let it free he slumped his dome, and never thought he'd raise it again, until, teary eyed and crazed, he gazed up to the crypt's quarter cocked window to see the first dawn of spring was here, and he looked at his dead father, and his jawbone slacked south to the linoleum floor as a winged ball of light came out of the hole in his father's head, and it seemed to peer up at him — deep in the optics — before drifting out the window crack and falling from sight.

More by the author:

THE ASPHODEL (2020)

A NOCTURNE FOR END TIMES (2020)

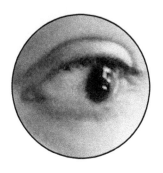

Lightning Source UK Ltd.
Milton Keynes UK
UKHW010628210621
385893UK00002B/340

9 781006 859236